Where This Trilogy of Novellas Began . . .

Hello, y'all!

In my 1996 novel, *A Place to Call Home*, five-year-old Claire, the precocious, southern-fried daughter of Dunderry, Georgia's most prosperous and respectable family, defied society to take up for ten-year-old Roan Sullivan—the abused, ragtag son of the town's most notorious drunk.

Their childhood devotion survived betrayal, tragedy and separation, but a lingering family scandal threatened them when they reunited as adults. Roan harbored a grim secret. The exposure of that secret and the resolution of the resulting drama united Claire's family in deep respect for Roan's devotion not only to Claire, but to them.

When we last saw Roan and Claire, they were preparing for a happy life together at last. Now, *Where the Foxgloves Bloom* brings readers back to Claire and Roan's lives (in 1997, two years after the end of the original story,) for a look at the joys and challenges they face in their early married years, when the arrival of a shocking stranger turns their world upside down again.

Because readers have such strong feelings of affection for Roan and Claire's story, I want to listen carefully to their input. That's why I'm presenting this sequel in three parts, all priced inexpensively, in ebook only. Part Two will come out in Summer 2014 and Part Three in Fall 2014.

Please send your opinion at deborahsmithauthor@gmail.com, and post your (good?) reviews at Amazon.com.

Thank you and, as always, I hope my books are worth your time and money.

Fondly,
—*Deb*

March 2014

The Novels of Deborah Smith

A Place To Call Home

The Crossroads Café

The Biscuit Witch

The Pickle Queen

A Gentle Rain

Alice At Heart

On Bear Mountain

Sweet Hush

Stone Flower Garden

Charming Grace

Miracle

Blue Willow

Silk and Stone

Short Stories:

The Yarn Spinner

Saving Jonquils

Click here for Deborah's Amazon Author Page

Where the Foxgloves Bloom

A Novella

Part one of a trilogy of sequels to *A Place to Call Home*

by

Deborah Smith

Copyright

Where The Foxgloves Bloom
A Novella
ISBN 978-1500228699

Cover design: Deborah Smith
Interior design: Hank Smith
Photo/artwork credits
Foxglove Flowers (Pink cluster, also Yellow cluster)© Le-thuy Do | Dreamstime.com
Mountain background (Sunny Cades Cove) © Jane Mortimore | Dreamstime.com
Old wood fence © Wyoosumran | Dreamstime.com
Golden shamrock © Rceeh | Dreamstime.com
Other Foxglove flowers © Elena Luria | Dreamstime.com
Rural English path © Chris Lofty | Dreamstime.com

Welcome to Dunderry

DUNDERRY, Georgia

The small southern town with the big Irish heart.

Founded 1838 by Irish immigrants

County seat of Dunderry County, "Gateway to the Mountain Tops"

Dunderry County is the second smallest county in Georgia at 123 square miles (smallest is Clarke County, 121 square miles home of University of Georgia) Dunderry County is located in the extreme north Georgia mountains between Fannin and Union Counties. Nearly half (60 square miles) of Dunderry County is protected wilderness. Dunderry County's mountains belong to the Cohutta range, one of the oldest mountain ranges on earth. The Cohuttas are part of the great east coast mountain chain including the Appalachians, the Blue Ridges, and the Smokies.

1997 Dunderry population: 3,000 city, 6,000 county

Primary Economy: Chicken and cattle farming, other agriculture including Christmas trees; tourism

Attractions: hiking, kayaking, fishing, hunting, other wilderness sports

Major Events: Dunderry St. Patrick's Day Festival, one of the top ten St. Patrick's Day festivals in the southeast U.S.

1

GRANDMA DOTTIE'S foxgloves were in bloom when Roan was sent away. "We'll make some magic with them, Claire," Grandpa Joe said. He thought Roan would come back some day if there were foxgloves up here on Dunshinnog to soften his step. I helped Grandpa plant them in the soft earth of the meadow. They are strong, because they have Irish fairies to watch over them. Even left alone on a mountaintop, they always come back.
—*From* A Place to Call Home

IN MY FAMILY, babies and secrets are like white sugar and strong iced tea: Potent when brewed together.

Nana said you bought tampons this week, Aunt Claire. Great Aunt Jane told her at the drug store. Not preggers yet, huh?

Not preggers, no. And everyone knew it. In the high-tech world of 1997, portable phones made it easier for the entire Maloney and Delaney clan and everyone else in Dunderry to trade constant updates on the possibility that one of Roan's sperm had speared one of my eggs. When I stopped picking up my birth control pills at the Dunderry Pharmacy Mama and my aunts heard immediately through a deeply rooted kudzu vine of informants. Then they started tracking my tampon purchases. Ethics, schmethics. If you want privacy, move to a place with subways and high rise apartments.

Dunderry, Georgia was still a picturesque, two-stoplight town surrounded by protective mountains, still just a dot on the map above the big star of Atlanta, a town where the churches, Kiwanis, Jaycees and Woman's Club banded together to maintain handsome welcome signs at all the major entry points, each sign bearing the town crest—a shamrock before a silhouette of mountains—and the slogan we still lived by:

A small southern town with a big Irish heart.

We tried to keep our focus small, but the world was changing. We, along with the rest of the planet, whirled toward the millennium with all the grace of Tonya Harding trying to kneecap Nancy Kerrigan at the Olympics, but we tried our best not to lose what made our part of the world strong and loving and dependable. And we tried our best not to alienate each other in the process.

Roan and I thought we'd made our peace with the past. We looked forward to the future. Our days were crammed with plans, work, love. In fact, we looked to the future with too much confidence, the way people do when they think they've survived their share of challenges and therefore life owes them nothing but cookies and cream from now on.

Which is why we didn't see Zach Donovan coming.

CRAFT BOOTHS and food concessions lined Main Street. The 5K Luck of the Irish road race had just ended. My aunt Rhonda Maloney was making my forty year old cousin Dwayne, Jr. drum an Irish *bodhran*, just as he had every year since he was twelve, in front of Mt. Gilead Methodist's *Southern Stuffed Irish Potatoes Get 'Em Here* fundraising tent. When Dwayne, Jr. was twelve (and I was, correspondingly, four,) the St. Patrick's Day Festival had been held in the arbor at the Methodist campground. Attendance then numbered in the hundreds, and the main entertainment was watching the children of Dunderry tap dance or clog to country-western music, badly. Now the festival occupied the entire downtown Dunderry square, and thousands of visitors drove in from all over northern Georgia.

But the humiliation of our local children remained the main entertainment.

On the festival stage across from the historic Dunderry courthouse, now a museum of mountain culture, my brother Josh stood handsomely in his green golf shirt and tailored slacks among the green bunting, the microphones, his campaign advisors, and a herd of miserable kids, most of them my nieces, nephews and first cousins once removed. All were dressed in "authentic" Irish costumes for their upcoming Irish stepdance performance.

Josh's new wife, Karen, directed a professional video photographer to take the best publicity footage of Josh for future campaign commercials. The photos, strategically angled from below stage level, would make Josh appear to tower wisely over the entire state of Georgia, and would, conveniently, cut out all but the most scenic account of blue sky, mountains, and folksy, Victorian rooftops.

No glimpses of us hillbillies.

Josh's daughter, my favorite niece, Amanda, glared at her stepmother then looked over the crowd at me. Her freckled face, a mirror of mine at twelve, was compressed in surly resignation. Poor kid. Her red hair bobbed in corkscrew curls beneath a wreath of silk shamrocks and fake roses. Her embroidered Celtic dress flopped like a green and gold dish towel around her skinny thighs. She dug one toe of her hard black stepdance taps into the stage floor, as if trying to find the escape hatch.

Shit, Amanda mouthed at me.

I put my hand over my heart in sympathy. *Been there, tapped that.*

"As Dunderry's state senator," my middle-aged brother boomed into a mike, "I welcome you all to the best St. Patty's Day festival in the southeast, presented by Dunderry, Georgia, my hometown, where our Irish heritage is as dear to us as the moonlight in our magnolias. I hope you'll all be back next year when I'm running for governor." Karen whooshed her hands at the family. *Applaud. LOUDLY.*

"We're not auditioning for a TV game show," I called.

Dozens of Maloneys and our Delaney kin frowned my way as they dutifully applauded. But Dr. Matthew Sullivan, and his wife, Dr. Tweet Sullivan, hid their smiles behind a pair of mixed-lab puppies they'd just adopted from the Humane Society booth. Mama shook her head at me. *Behave.* Daddy was too involved positioning his video cam to notice. Grandma Dottie, parked in a wheelchair near the stage, gave me a thumbs-up. Various aunts, uncles, and cousins of varying degrees shushed me then returned to their camera-ready positions. My family took more pictures of each other than Japanese tourists visiting Disneyland. They had pixels to capture.

I was testy, I admit it. Roan and I had been swimming upstream to spawn for exactly six months that day, with no results. I was scared. As a rule, Maloneys procreate faster than lovesick salmon. My brothers were baby-making machines. Brady had five children, Hop and Evan had eleven between them, and Josh, who had only been married briefly before his first wife died, had Amanda from that union and Matthew from his fling with Sally McClendon.

Depressed, I looked away from the happy crowd. One of my staff photographers waved at me from the sidewalk in front of the *Dunderry Weekly Shamrock's* offices. I waved back and grabbed a cell phone from my jeans pocket. "Don't take any more pictures of my brother Josh. I don't care how much his wife insists."

"Okay, boss. But she's dogging me."

"She's heading your way. *Run.*"

The photographer ducked inside the newspaper office. Karen frowned and followed him inside. They disappeared behind my proud promotional banner in the front window.

NOW ONLINE! DAILY NEWS AND WEATHER
AT *www.dunderryshamrock.com.*

My new website had provoked a good deal of eye-rolling among family and friends. "No one wants to read their news off a computer, Sis," Brady said patiently. "This website stuff is just a passing fad. There's no profit in it."

I sighed. Riverdance music blared from speakers on the stage. The costumed boys and girls stiffened their shoulders, clamped their arms to their sides, and began the half-graceful, half-ludicrous prancing that vaguely simulated classic Irish step dancing. Amanda stomped on her cousin Sheri's foot, and Sheri lost her balance and stomped on her cousin Eldon's foot, and the domino effect went into action. Dozens of awkward Maloney and Delaney spawn were soon tromping all over one another's toes.

Ah, tradition.

Violet and Rebecca, my dearest girl cousins, turned from filming their hapless kids. Both made elaborately pained faces at me. They remembered my hard toes and their injured ones.

I mouthed, *Who me*?

Time to leave the scene of the crime. I headed toward a row of two-story country stores linked by a long balcony. The upstairs had been converted to offices, and Roan now owned the building. Everyone had been surprised and pleased when Roan left the historic name plaque on it. *Delaney Hall.* I myself had told him to rename it *Sullivan Hall*, but we both knew if he did Mama's kin would spit in his gravy at the next family reunion.

I climbed the aged front stairs, deliberately clumping my mules on the whitewashed wood, then delicately rattling the glass door of the office suite. I stepped inside. The soft twang of Woody Guthrie's voice curled from a CD player. *This land is your land, this land is my land.* Roan could recite the lyrics to almost all of Guthrie's songs, and had them all on CD. When we ditched our birth control I gave him a set of Guthrie's children's songs.

Polished wood creaked gently beneath my feet. Light streamed in through wavy glass of tall windows. Roan had removed the ceiling's aging plaster board to expose handsome, rough-hewn beams. The feel was open and inviting and clean. A scattering of desks, phones, computers, printers, and overstuffed bookcases showed where his two-person staff worked.

DBA Rathcabhain Inc. the business license said. Old Irish for 'fortress of the hollow.' Only a few of us knew what that meant to Roan, and why. He had grown up in a tiny trailer in a junk-strewn hollow not far from my family's farm. Now he bought foreclosures in bad neighborhoods, restored them and sold the renovated homes to low-income families. At the moment his crew was refurbishing a dozen small homes on Atlanta's southside.

I thrust out my breasts, primped my red ponytail, and sashayed into his office. "You promised to come down for the annual stomping of Maloney and Delaney adolescent toes."

Roan Sullivan, my husband of two years, my love since childhood, looked up from a drafting table strewn with blueprints. At 37 he had matured into a glorious man, tall and broad-shouldered. His black hair was wavy and coarse and would never quite behave, which I loved. Some people claimed he smiled like a wolf, but his gray eyes gleamed with welcome as he looked at me. I loved his smile, but it was never quite enough to lift the aura of isolation around him. "I said I *might*."

"Roan."

"I'm sorry. You know I hate this festival."

"Yes, but . . ." I stood there studying him as he studied me. Not giving an inch, either of us. "If we ever have kids, they'll have to dance in Aunt Gloria's St. Patty's Day recital. Bad dancing is a tradition. And you'll *have* to stand by the stage and take pictures of them being humiliated. Just like you watched me when we were kids."

"I had plenty of irresistible reasons for watching *you*, Peep."

My old nickname. "Don't flatter me, boy. I'm not a pushover."

I lied. He could see it. He walked toward me, looking me over, pausing at the good spots. I gave him the same scrutiny. His hand slid into his khakis' front pocket. He drew out a small, velvet box. "A leprechaun left this for you."

"Roan."

"I can't help it. Old habit."

He'd given me my first shamrock charm when we were kids. I opened the box gently. There lay a delicate shamrock in filigreed gold with a small ruby at the center. "This makes number twenty. I love it, but *stop*. I'll have to get a second charm bracelet or start wearing them as piercings." I held the tiny charm to the top of my ear. "What do you think? Right there. Or here." I pulled up the front of my sweater and held the charm by my navel. "I'll get my navel pierced. Or hey, I know." I unzipped my jeans, angled a forefinger under the band of my panties, and began easing the material down. "I'll have a more *intimate* part pierced . . ."

He laughed. "All right, it's a deal."

I slid my hands up his shoulders, the sides of his neck, his jaw, and into his hair. He bent me backwards over his arm. We kissed, meeting halfway, a good balance. Sometimes, when he was too deep inside him, it was as if he reached for me through the bars of a cell. He thought his father was there, parts of him, undisciplined, violent, a drunk. He had to lock him up.

A beeping sound interrupted us. Roan frowned past me at the security console on one wall. Someone had come in through the back door. It led down a narrow set of service stairs to a tiny alley between the Delaney block and the two-story building where my great-great uncle Neeco Maloney started selling Chevrolets in 1935.

Neeco's old Chevy dealership was now an antique mall run by his great-great granddaughter and namesake, Neecette. Neecette had gated the alley a year earlier to keep skateboarders off the alley's speedy concrete walkway. No one could get into that alley without a key, much less the back door of Roan's offices.

Stay here, he mouthed. Then he took a golf club from one corner and slipped from the office. Roan didn't play golf, but Brady kept trying to lure him to the Dunderry Country Club for a lesson. Thus, the loan of a nine iron, in case Roan ever gave into a sudden whim to join Brady at the driving range.

I counted to ten, gave up at five, then followed Roan.

I heard the quick thud of his heavy leather walking shoes on the old wood floor. Then the teeth-jarring slam of the nine iron hitting metal.

A deep male drawl rose in a hoarse yelp. "*Fuck, man*!"

"Back off," Roan said softly. "If I meant to hit you, I would have. And I will, next time."

I rushed through a doorway and halted. Roan stood on one side of a block of low file cabinets. The small room was jammed with kayaks hanging from the wall and ceiling, plus strangely disembodied wetsuits, canoe paddles, backpacks, nylon rock-climbing ropes, and cases of something called TrailPro, a high protein granola bar for serious hikers. Cohutta Outdoors, a test banner said. One of our business ventures, still in the planning stages. Atop the waist-high file cabinets lay the office's lockbox, where Roan stored several thousand dollars in petty cash.

The box now bore a deep dent in the shape of the nine iron. A bottom drawer of the file cabinet stood open. A brawny hand wavered over the cash box, either determined to save the snatch-and-grab opportunity or too damned scared of Roan to move.

My eyes rose to the hand's owner.

He was young, maybe early twenties. As tall as Roan, with thick shoulders and a thick jaw. His arm muscles were ropey and veined, covered in tattoos. His skin was pale but freckled, as if something had strained the sunlight out of him. He wore a faded *Grateful Dead* t-shirt and jeans speckled with bleach stains. His dark-brown hair bristled in an ugly buzz cut. He could have been handsome in better circumstances, but not like this.

His startled gaze shifted to me then hardened and shifted back to Roan. "I'm taking this fucking money, man. I've got a kid to take care of. I need the money."

"Right. A kid. Sure."

"It's true. I'm takin' it."

"I'll break every bone in your body."

"Roan, let him go," I said quietly. "It's just money."

"He can walk out. Fine. But not with anything that belongs to *me*."

"Fuck, man. Listen to your babe." But he stepped back warily. *Thank God*, I thought. Then he whipped a hand behind him and pulled a gun from the waistband of his jeans.

He pointed it at Roan's chest. "All right, man, now you've pissed me off. Put the fuckin' golf club down and let me have that box. Or I'll shoot your motherfuckin' heart out."

"Roan," I said. "*Roan.*"

Roan lowered the golf club to the desk. "Let my wife walk out the front door. *Now.*"

"Sure. She can go. I don't hurt no women."

"Claire. *Go.*"

"No. I'm sorry. But *no.*" This stranger could take Roan away from me. "No one's going to hurt you," I said quietly. "Take the money. Go. Go on, now. It's okay. Just walk out. Please. Go on now. *Shoo.*"

The stranger stared at me. *Shoo*? What could he say to *that*? He snatched the lockbox to his chest, tucked the gun in the waistband of his jeans, then backed toward the door.

Relief eased the tourniquet around my lungs. We'd been robbed, but it was over. In another few seconds this stranger would be out the door and gone—

Roan charged him.

The two of them went down in a swinging cluster of fists. I dodged them, yelling. When Roan threw the young guy against a wall, the gun fell to the floor. I grabbed it.

I know my way around a trigger. After all, I grew up in a family who loved guns with a Second Amendment zeal second only to sex and football. Maloneys and Delaneys give guns as shower gifts. *Baby* shower gifts.

I clamped both hands around the stock, kept my finger off the trigger, and tested the safety latch with my thumb. It was open. By now Roan and the stranger were slugging each other into the front room. They hit the suite's front door and it burst outward, dumping them onto the balcony that overlooked Main Street. I rushed after them, aiming the gun here and there, my finger posed on the trigger.

Roan rammed the young guy's face into a post. The stranger spit blood then elbowed Roan in the face. Blood spewed from Roans' nose. This fight was now far beyond a brawl. It was sadistic. I pointed the pistol at the stranger's torso. I finally had a clear shot.

I pulled the trigger.

An empty click.

I pulled the trigger again.

Nothing.

The gun wasn't even loaded.

Roan drove a fist into the stranger's stomach. He dodged the crippling punch at the last minute but Roan still got him in the ribs. He groaned. I heard bones crack.

Our visitor went backwards over the balcony with a denimed *whoosh* of blue jeaned legs. He landed on the peaked canvas roof of Mt. Gilead's potato tent, which was staffed by my Aunt Arnetta and about a dozen other Maloneys and Delaneys.

The tent collapsed. Tables crashed and flipped, spilling mountains of twice-bakes and home fries. People tumbled over each other, stomping squeeze bottles of cheese, mustard and ketchup. Obscene splats of condiment color squirted onto the aged pavement of downtown Dunderry's finest street.

Up on the stage, Amanda and the other kids screamed and scattered, their tap shoes making a chaotic rattle on the plywood. The *Riverdance* music stopped abruptly and the microphones gurgled. Josh, Daddy and the other men of my family began bulldozing their way through the thong, with Mama yelling for Alvin Tobbler, our sheriff. Since Alvin had been filming his daughter, Cherice, on stage, he was nearby.

Everyone else reached for a cell phone or a concealed weapon. *Dunderry: Armed and ready.* Our unofficial slogan.

The tent, the taters, and my relatives' dignity were a total loss. Roan, his hands and face bleeding, his breath coming in ragged gulps, staggered to the balcony rail. I grabbed him by one arm to steady him. "Look at me. Roan. Look at me. Look at me. Let me see you."

He braced himself against a balcony post. I tried not to wince at the cuts, the split lip, the swelling cheekbone. I finally recognized him behind the hard gray mirrors of his eyes. I made a hoarse sound. "Thank God."

We leaned over the balcony rail. Our robber sprawled on his back in a lumpy bed of green-and-white canvas, half-atop an overturned drink cooler that spilled ice and watery slush from beneath the crushed tent. He moaned and shifted weakly.

A pink baby booty protruded from the front pocket on his jeans.

"Claire. Claire Karleen." Suddenly I realized Mama and Daddy were yelling up at me. "Are you and Roan all right? Stay there, we're coming." They pushed their way toward the lower staircase, with all of my brothers, nieces, nephews, cousins, aunts and uncles crowding up behind them, a hearty plaid of red and brown hair over ruddy faces, all those outraged Maloney and Delaney eyes switching from the carnage of the tent to the carnage of Roan's face, staring up at him.

His face turned hard and sad, and then he looked away from the unwanted audience. "You know what they're thinking," he said hoarsely.

Yes, I knew. Another St. Patrick's Day spectacle. Another violent and public incident featuring *him.* I wound my arm around his shoulders and bent my head close to his. No use reminding him he wasn't ten years old or that this mess wasn't his fault, then or now. "I'm here," I whispered, cupping my hand beneath his bleeding knuckles. "Just like then. Still here."

He closed bloody fingers around my palm.

2

DUNDERRY REGIONAL Hospital had only been open a year, and most of that time had been devoted to ceremonies naming various rooms, wings and hallways after esteemed members of my family. Maloneys and Delaneys had, after all, been instrumental in the Dunderry Hospital Authority.

The builders included *Hop & Evan Maloney Brothers Construction* (my favorite brothers had no imagination for corporate names) and *BAM Development* (because Brady Alton Maloney had gotten all our family marketing genes.) Mama's brother, Dr. Mallory Delaney, had overseen the staffing choices and now chaired the board. Aunt Bess Maloney headed social services.

My cousin Violet, a physical therapist, was a senior staff member in the rehab department, and cousin Rebecca and her mother, Aunt Jane, ran the volunteer auxiliary. Josh had dipped his senatorial hand deep into the state's pork barrel to fund lots of extras, such as the *Joseph Maloney Community Room.* Grandpa Joe would have preferred a pipe-smoking lounge in his honor, but never mind.

The "regional" part was debatable, since the hospital only boasted fifty beds, but the facilities proudly included a maternity ward, a surgical suite, and two intensive care units, one for general purposes and the other for cardiac cases. The grand little hospital stood atop a hill just outside town. It was a warm box of red brick and silvery granite, accented with a series of peaked brick façades around the perimeter of the roof. Depending on your point of view, the faux rooftop achieved the old-fashioned appeal of a historic building. Or else we had run out of money to finish the top floor.

Down on the bottom floor, our battered stranger lay handcuffed in an exam room, guarded by two deputies. They kept a hornet's nest of angry Dunderry citizens, most of them my family, from strangling him.

I made the rounds from one small crisis to another. Injured Methodists were being patched up in the ER. Daddy was being treated for what we hoped were just stress-induced chest pains. Mama sat between him and Grandma Dottie in an exam room, holding his hand on one side and hers on the other.

Tweet, seven months' pregnant, had fainted while tending Roan's face during the drive to the hospital. She was now up in the maternity ward with electrodes on her chest and belly. Matthew sat beside her, holding her hand and staring intently at the monitors with her.

"How's Bigger?" Matthew asked grimly. Tweet merely waved a hand at me. She wouldn't take her eyes off the screens.

Bigger. Matthew had called Roan that affectionate nickname since childhood, a substitute for father or brother, since Roan was both and neither.

"He says he'll be up here as soon as the doctors finish reattaching everything. By the way, your dad'll be up here in a minute, too."

"You mean Josh?" Matthew corrected me with a stony smile. He and my oldest brother had a rocky father-son relationship. After all, they'd only met two years ago, and their bonding process hadn't gone as well as we'd hoped.

I sighed. "Josh and Karen are downstairs telling an Atlanta correspondent for CNN about the 'get-tough-on-crime' policy he'll support when he's governor. Karen sees this incident as a good chance for Josh to demonstrate his leadership. In the meantime, she pushed Amanda off on Hop and Luanne. Amanda's mad, as usual."

"Damn." Matthew and his baby sister, well, half-sister, were close. "I'll check on her."

"Good. She's in the lobby with everyone else. Hear that furious bzzzz? The entire Maloney-Delaney hive is about to erupt. Alvin may have to put another deputy at our criminal's door. The guy's probably terrified."

"You're sympathetic? He had a gun. He could've—"

"I don't think he's vicious. I think he's desperate."

"Look, Bigger raised me to look past appearances, but right now I feel like throwing that guy under a train. If anything happens to Tweet and the baby because of him . . ."

Tweet prodded his arm. "Matthew, ssssh." She'd been too engrossed the monitors to comment before. "We're fine. I don't deal well with the sight of wounded humans, that's all. Wounded dogs, cats, horses, cows, pigs, hamsters—no problem. But the sight of Roan's battered face flipped me out. But really, hon, I'm fine, now. And so is our little fetal Tweety bird." Tweet grinned and patted her stomach then pointed at a monitor. "Look there. See? Heart rate, rhythm, both fine. If I were a pregnant Holstein I'd be heading back out to the pasture to munch some alfalfa by now."

Matthew chortled. "If you were a pregnant Holstein I'd be in jail for Holstein-love. And for selling our story to the *National Enquirer.*"

She laughed. I patted Matthew's shoulder, enviously kissed Tweet's giant, bare belly, then hurried back down to the ER. After another quick check of Daddy and the others I rushed back to Roan's cubicle, where Uncle Mallory was finishing the final touches on his stitches. Roan sat sideways on a gurney with his long legs dangling and his ice-packed hands on a tray table. "Okay?" he managed to ask through swollen lips.

"Yes. Tweet, Matthew, their baby, Daddy, the Methodists, everyone."

"I hope the criminal who did this to Roan isn't 'okay,'" Uncle Mallory said darkly. He stood back to admire his work. One set of stitches resembled an inch-long zipper at the right corner of Roan's mouth, and the other made a tiny, cross-pole gate across his left eyebrow.

Uncle Cully Delaney waved goodbye to us from the doorway. "Rinse your mouth out every two hours and take your antibiotics, Roan." Though retired from active practice, Mama's dentist-brother had dropped in to glue and wire one of Roan's lower molars back into place.

Roan scowled but gave him a thumbs up. He had issues about his teeth. As a kid, "snaggle tooth" had been one of many taunts he heard. He angled his head toward me. I knew what he wanted me to say about his tooth.

"Looks as good as new."

"How about the rest of my face?"

"I love you."

"That bad?"

I managed a smile. He would heal. Nothing else mattered. I adjusted the cold pack wrapped around his right hand. "As soon as you get a splint on that broken finger I'll take you home."

Mama stuck her head in. "Your Daddy's been cleared. His EKG turned out fine. They gave him a pill for nerves, and I made them give me one, too. Your grandma turned down a pill for herself. She has five Marlboros in her sweater that she thinks we don't know about. When we get to the farm I'll pour her a double bourbon and let her smoke in the kitchen."

Grandma Dottie was eighty five. Mama and Daddy were nearly seventy. My elders weren't immortal anymore. I didn't want to lose them. "I *knew* Daddy was just having an anxiety attack." Empty bravado. I tried to sound confident.

Her eyes flashed. "Oh, he's back to his cocky old self. He and your brothers want to skin that thug alive. I agree. What's the world coming to?" She looked at Roan grimly. "Roan, I wish you'd finished him off. God help me. But I do wish you'd killed him."

She went to Roan and kissed the top of his head. I flinched. Roan's jaw hardened and I saw the unhappiness in his eyes. She meant it as a compliment, but to him she was referencing his past. The boy who was capable of killing.

My clueless, bloodthirsty mama hugged me then hustled away to check on Daddy again. She brushed a smear of Roan's iodine off her tailored green blouse, which was covered in an heirloom collection of leprechaun pins and buttons. Our St. Patrick's Day was ending in an orange patina of antiseptic.

Alvin stepped into the room. Big and brawny, with the beginnings of a hard gut protruding over his big silver belt buckle, he had a jaw like a bulldog's and a voice deep enough to sing the bass part in "Elvira." Alvin Tobbler was the quintessential image of a small town Southern sheriff.

Except for the fact that he was the first black sheriff in Dunderry's history. He nodded to Uncle Mallory. "Doc."

Uncle Mallory nodded back. "Sheriff."

Alvin gave Roan a grimly satisfied nod. "Your boxing partner has a couple of cracked ribs, a fractured nose, and a mild concussion. Plus lots of stitches here and there. Congratulations. I'd say you banged him up worse than he banged you. You won."

Roan squinted. "Doesn't feel like it."

"Has the guy told you anything about himself?" I asked Alvin.

"No, but I've run his records." Alvin pulled a notepad from his shirt pocket and flipped it open. "Let's see. He's six-four, one-hundred-ninety pounds, age twenty-two. Last known address: Chattanooga, Tennessee. He's been in and out of trouble since he was eighteen and has a juvenile record to prove it. Minor drug dealing, assault, multiple burglaries, check fraud, disturbing the peace, et cetera. He just got out of prison in Tennessee about a week ago."

"A violent drug dealer!" Uncle Mallory growled. "I never thought we'd have that kind of problem in Dunderry. By God, we need to send a strong message to the community about this. Throw the book at this no-account."

Alvin nodded. "And here's the icing on the cake." He held out his notebook. "He's got this tattooed on the inside of his right forearm."

Alvin had sketched three stars in a vertical line. Inside the top star was the letter C. Inside the middle star was a W. In the bottom star, an M.

Roan went very still. Uncle Mallory said, "What's that mean?"

"It's a gang symbol," I explained dully. "The Council of White Men."

"Oh, my lord. That's one of those racist gangs, isn't it?"

"Yes."

When my uncle stared at Alvin with the brand of well-intentioned sympathy that most people of color view as pity, Alvin sighed and turned to leave. "Yeah, well. More news as I get it."

"Wait," I said. "A name. What's this guy's name? Sorry, it's the newspaper editor in me. You gave us the what, how and why. I need a 'who.'"

Alvin grunted. "Zachary Donovan. How's that for an Irish moniker? Maybe that's why he dropped in here on St. Patrick's Day. No luck of the Irish for him, though."

Zachary Donovan. Only twenty-two but well on his way to a life as a career criminal. Yet he'd seemed more intent on escaping from Roan than assaulting him. He'd carried an unloaded gun. And I kept thinking of the pink knitted bootie in his jeans' pocket.

Freddie Delaney, one of Alvin's junior deputies, poked his brown-haired head through the doorway. "Sorry to interrupt, Sheriff. But the uh, prisoner, has a request."

Alvin pivoted slowly, with extreme patience. My cousin Freddie wasn't cut out to be a law officer. He'd wanted to play bluegrass fiddle and tour the festival circuit for a (meager) living. He'd had a band. But he'd also had a girlfriend in the band. She played mandolin on stage and Freddie's skin flute in private. So now they had a mortgage, a marriage license, and a one-year old.

"Prisoners don't get to have requests, Freddie," Alvin said patiently.

"I just thought I should tell you, sir. He, uh, he wants to talk to Claire."

Uncle Mallory gaped at him. "What? *What*? Freddie, you came over here to tell us that nonsense? No. Tell him no. Hell, no."

Freddie gulped. "Uncle Mallory, I, uh, I . . ."

"I'll take care of this," Alvin growled.

"Wait," I said.

Roan swiveled toward me. "Not going . . ." He struggled with his damaged mouth. "to happen."

I touched his arm. We didn't order each other around. At least, not in public. "Did he say why he wants to see me?" I asked Freddie.

Freddie turned paler. Delaneys tend to be fair-skinned, unlike ruddy Maloneys. "Uh, no. He just said, 'Can you get Julia Roberts in here?' And I said, 'I wish.' And he said, 'The redhead. The wife. I need to ask her something.'"

Roan pulled his hand free from the cold pack, shoved the tray table aside, and started to get off the gurney. I stepped in front him. "Please. The guy's injured. He's handcuffed to a bed. He can't hurt me. Alvin and Freddie will stand at the door and keep an eye on me. All right? I want to talk to him."

"*Why*?"

"Journalistic curiosity. Call it an interview. I own the newspaper. It's my job to ask questions."

"Claire."

"I'll be right back. I can handle this. I've handled worse." He knew what I meant. When I worked at a big paper down in Florida I'd nearly been killed trying to help a woman get away from her abusive ex-husband. She'd died but I'd lived, though I'd always have scars on my right leg as a reminder. Roan exhaled. Through gritted teeth he finally managed, "I go too. No other way. All right?"

I kissed his forehead. Marriage is about compromise. Okay, in Dunderry, marriage is about pretending to compromise in front of your nosy uncle, your gossipy cousin and your discreetly curious other cousin, the sheriff.

"All right," I said, and helped Roan stand up.

As we walked out Uncle Mallory threw up both hands and said, "Claire Karleen, I swear! You just can't leave trouble alone."

Some things never change.

The exam rooms shared a large communal area. I had to navigate Roan through a tribe of my relatives and other bandaged, irate citizens. When the testy group realized Roan and I was headed for Zach Donovan's deputy-enhanced doorway they uttered a collective gasp followed by agitated stares and outright protests.

"Claire, have you lost your mind?"

"Mallory must have knocked Roan out with some morphine. Roan, how can you let your wife do this?"

Roan cushioned his broken-fingered hand closer to his chest as if I'd threatened to squeeze it.

My Aunt Dottie huffed loudly. "That criminal ruined our festival, put us in the emergency room, and now he has the gall to demand a meeting with the people he tried to rob. This is what comes of taking prayer out of the schools!"

"Hold on," Alvin said as I reached the door to Donovan's room. He waved two deputies aside then turned to me. I was suddenly eye-level with a human wall of badge, khaki and polished nickel nameplate. "Claire, you alert me if he says one wrong word. Promise?"

"If his mouth is as swollen as Roan's he'll be lucky to say any word at all."

"Five minutes."

I nodded.

Alvin stepped aside.

I took a deep breath as Roan and I entered the small, brightly lit room. Zach Donovan was a frightening but also pathetic sight. His head was perched awkwardly on a small pillow. His eyes were swollen slits. His upper lip had puffed out so badly I could see the soft pink underside. Sutures made ugly black zippers on his eyebrows and cheekbones.

He wore only his jeans, and a white sheet had been tossed haphazardly over his midsection. His cracked ribcage was bound from nipples to stomach with heavy white tape. Swaths of his brown chest hair were smeared with orangey streaks of iodine. Someone had tossed his dirty jogging shoes in a corner. His bare feet were big, pale and vulnerable looking. Wide straps bound each blue-jeaned ankle to the gurney. His long, bare arms were handcuffed to the gurney by his thighs.

He didn't look at us. He stared at the ceiling. I could see just the barest gleam of his eyes between the raw muffins of his eyelids. One eye looked like a ball of raw tuna at a sushi bar. The other was angry.

Roan blocked me with one arm, but I shook my head at him. We traded silent communication. *Yes. No. It's all right. Please.*

He lowered his arm.

I walked over to Donovan slowly. The gang tattoo stood out on the inside of his right forearm, among a nest of cobras. The tattoos that covered both arms to his shoulders included skulls, daggers, and naked women. Tattoos were no big deal. The usual macho stuff. My uncle Ralph Maloney, an Atlanta lawyer and president of the *Bikers Born To Litigate Club*, had a skull tattoo on his left butt check now. So Daddy and my other uncles claimed.

But Donovan's Council of White Men tattoo was something else. It had been crudely etched, like the blurred pattern on a piece of old flow-blue china. As a big-city reporter down in Florida I'd written a few stories about prison life. Inmates built illicit tattoo guns with motors taken from hair dryers and fans; their needles were often no more than the sharpened wires from paper clips; their tattoo ink came from cheap writing pens.

This was a prison tattoo. An ugly pucker of pink scar tissue traced one of the stars in Donovan's racist gang symbol. Infection and prison tats went hand in ungloved hand.

"Hello, Zach," I said quietly. "Nice to meet you. Let's be formal. My name's Claire. This is Roan. We're Claire and Roan Sullivan. I'll do most of the talking, since both you and my husband aren't in much condition to form words."

He continued to stare at the ceiling. His swollen lips moved slowly. His voice was a soft rasp. "You ain't scared of the big, bad wolf?"

"If you knew better, you should be scared of *me*, dude." I laid a hand on his bare arm, and he flinched.

"Claire," Roan growled.

"Relax, both of you. I'm going to straighten this sheet and fix the pillow." I fluffed and organized the starched cover, folding it across Donovan so he was demurely covered from neck to knees. Next I lifted his head gently and set his pillow at a comfortable angle. "There." I pulled up a chair and sat down close enough to smell his sweat and antiseptic. Roan stepped to the foot of gurney, looming over us. He wanted Donovan to know I had protection.

Donovan's eyes flickered. He finally shifted his gaze to us, glaring at Roan, then looking at me. "Why did you give me a chance . . . why'd you tell me to . . . just *shoo*?"

"I gave you the benefit of the doubt. A chance to walk away. You just didn't *shoo* fast enough. I knew my husband would—pardon me, but let's talk turkey, here. I knew he'd kick your ass."

"But then you tried to *shoot* me."

"Nobody elbows my husband in the face and walks away cheap. Why wasn't the gun loaded?"

"Like I said. Ain't never . . . hurt no woman."

"What about men? Would you shoot a *man*? Would you have shot my husband?"

He blinked slowly, painfully. His mouth quirked. "Not without bullets."

Irony? Humor? Or stupidity? Roan made a disgusted sound. I rubbed a line of tension in my forehead. "Okay, Zach. The sheriff isn't giving us much time for chitchat. Why do you want to talk to us?"

His throat worked. His unwavering stare returned to the ceiling. "I said I got a kid," he whispered. "I wasn't lyin'."

My spine tingled. "All right. I believe you."

"She ain't got nobody else . . . but me. Just a baby. And she's . . . sickly."

More prickles ran up my backbone. My God. "Where is she, Zach?"

He seemed to be struggling with every impulse. His silence was excruciating. *He hates trusting anyone, I thought. He's like Roan, that way.*

Roan stepped closer to the gurney. When I looked at him, his face was fierce. "Be a man. Do what's best for your kid."

Donovan's swollen eyes instantly swiveled to him, full of rage. "Fuck you, you rich asshole. What do *you* care?"

The air froze around Roan. Trouble. I stood quickly. "Zach, we'll make sure your baby's taken care of. You have my word. You have no choice here. *Where is she*?"

He deflated. His stare went back to the acoustic ceiling tile. "Dunderry . . . Motor Court. Room seven."

The motor court. God. The worst kind of run-down motel, a few miles outside town. I winced. The address was infamous, not just in general but in Roan's family history. Steckem Road. I touched Donovan's arm. "We'll go get her. She'll be all right. Don't worry."

"Yeah," he whispered hoarsely. "Right."

"Times up," Alvin boomed, stepping inside the room. He glared down at Zach. "I heard what he said. So Mr. Council of White Men says he left a baby at that rent-by-the-hour dive? I'll check it out." Alvin jerked the latch on one of Donovan's ankle straps. "Enjoy these fine, luxury accommodations tonight. Tomorrow you'll take up residence in the Dunderry County Jail. If you aren't lying about the baby, then you can thank Claire and Roan here for convincing you to do the decent thing for once in your life."

Donovan's horribly disfigured mouth curled in a small sneer. "Suck my dick, *nigger*."

Eeew yew. I squinted up at Alvin. His expression went frigid. But Alvin, a man of the world, who'd played linebacker for the *Dallas Cowboys*, didn't blink. He'd heard the word plenty of times, here, there, everywhere. It bounced off his dark skin like a ricocheting rock. Alvin pursed his lips into a smile. "You just lost your TV privileges for a week."

Alvin turned on a heel and strode from the room. Roan stared down at Zach, clearly hating him. I couldn't blame Roan. What a sad mix of misery, meanness, and frustration. "How's that death wish working out?" Roan asked him, his voice a rasp. "You're getting a lot of practice today."

Donovan strained at the handcuffs. "Shove it, you rich fuck. All you had to do was let me have the money."

"So you could drag your *baby* along with you while you robbed the next target? So you could *leave* her at another shitty motel where somebody might *hurt* her? This is your baby's lucky night. The sheriff's right. Telling us where to find her is the only thing you've done right so far."

I grasped Roan's arm. "That's enough. Let's go."

"Where'll they take her?" Donovan groaned.

I frowned at him. "I'm sure Sheriff Tobbler will place her with our local social services people. They'll put her in foster care . . . unless you want to rethink what you said about not having any family to call. Are you certain?"

The slits of Zach Donovan's raw eyes disappeared into the heavy folds of his swollen lids. He raised his head then banged it back hard onto the pillow. His bloodied hands clenched into helpless fists. "Yeah."

I exhaled wearily and tugged Roan toward the door.

"Wait," Donovan said hoarsely.

We looked back at him. "Yes?" I said.

"Blood sees after blood. You believe in that? I seen all your kin around here. Like a bunch of worried monkeys looking after one another. Family takes care of family?"

"Yes. I do believe in family." And yes, at times my clan resembled nothing so much as an overwrought tribe of chimps.

"I don't want my kid stuck with people who got no reason to want her."

"If you have relatives, then now's the time to tell us. Give us a name."

He stared at the ceiling angrily. "*Sullivan*," he whispered.

3

ROAN SAID ONLY two words after Zach Donovan told us he was the son of Steckum Road's notorious Daisy McClendon, who wisely had vacated the premises more than twenty years ago, right after Big Roan died.

"You're lying."

Then Roan walked out

Roan and I drove in stunned silence. I didn't know *what* to believe. Where Steckem Road and the McClendon sisters were concerned, anything was possible. My God. After what we'd been through resolving Matthew's tangled beginnings as the son of Daisy's baby sister, Sally.

"Are you all right?" I asked as we entered the dark, hilly woods north of town. Roan could barely grip his Jeep's steering wheel. In the blue-green light of the dash his face looked like a mask from a house of horrors.

He replied with a small, sharp gesture of his splinted hand. *Upset. Angry. No, I'm not all right.* "Want to settle this," he managed to say. "He's lying."

I sat back in the passenger seat, worried.

We turned off the main road at a battered green sign with bullet holes in it. Steckum Road. Better known, in our childhood, as *Stick 'Em In Road.* The four McClendon sisters's shabby houses were long gone, their foundations covered by kudzu, pines, and blackberry briars. But I could still picture them and every detail of what had happened there.

That Easter Sunday, when Roan and I were kids, we stood together, terrified, in the ugly, junk-filled yard of the McClendon shacks. I felt like a redheaded princess of Easter finery compared to Roan's shamed poverty. We watched with horrified curiosity as Mama and her sisters went inside some of the shacks to deliver Bible verses and Easter charity to the McClendon sister and their unsaved children. We didn't know it then, but Sally McClendon's baby boy, Matthew, was Josh's son.

Suddenly Sally's big sister, Daisy, ran out of her house wearing just a bra and cutoff jeans, her gold-plated hair tangled around her face.

One of her eyes was swollen shut. "You come get him, Roanie! You come get that son of a bitch outta my bed! I ain't gonna put up with his shit no more!"

The door slapped open and Big Roan staggered out, lopsided on his metal leg, bare-chested, the waistband of his trousers hanging unfastened beneath his hairy beer gut. His bloodshot eyes settled on me. Roan tried to get in front of me, like a shield, but I still felt the hate in his daddy's glare.

"Don't you hide your little fancy fluffball from me, boy. Her people ain't no better'n us. Specially her damned uncle and her—"

"Leave her be," Roan said through gritted teeth. "It ain't her fault she's rich."

"Someday the cock'll come home to crow, you little fluffball, right on your family's fine doorstep—"

Daisy got between Big Roan and us. "Big Roan, keep quiet! You want to get us all in trouble?"

Roan shoved his father. Outraged, Big Roan tried to strangle him. I used the only weapon I had. A hard-boiled Easter egg. I fast-balled it at Big Roan Sullivan's temple. God might not care about the McClendon sisters and their neglected children, but He cared enough to give me good aim on Roan's behalf. I knocked Big Roan out, cold.

Roan never forgot the violence and humiliation of that day. Easter became another holiday he'd rather not celebrate. Like so many unresolved conversations a married couple store in a soundproof chest, we didn't talk about it.

But it was there.

Whores and violence and Easter eggs. How we still thought of Steckem Road.

WE CLIMBED OUT of Roan's Jeep on the cracked concrete of the motor court's parking lot under the dim blue light of a *Dunderry Motor Court* sign so old it still advertised air conditioning as an option. A couple of aged cars and a muddy pick-up fronted the line of peeling doors and sagging awnings. The motel's current owner hugged herself outside the lit window of the number one unit. She lived there with her teenaged daughter and grandchild. She looked scared.

Alvin walked over from his patrol car. "Go on back inside, Miz Macy. We'll take care of this."

"I don't know nothing. He just rented the room this morning. Tiffany's in there, like I said on the phone. She don't know nothing neither. I'm glad to get rid of him. He was too good-looking to have around a teenager. And he was sweet to her. She's stupid about sweet men."

"Go on, now. We'll send her along."

The woman crept back inside, scowling.

I headed for a door that had a rusty seven on it. Roan moved quickly to block me. Adrenaline overcame the punched muscles, the stitches, the reset tooth, the splinted hand. "No."

Alvin stepped in front of us both, flipping the door key in his dark hand. "Claire, this is official business."

"There's a baby in that room."

"Maybe so, but I doubt it's a *Sullivan* baby. Donovan knows it'll take some time to check out his story about being Roan's half-brother. He's worried that I won't forget his big-mouthed name-calling. He thinks he might have a 'tragic accident' in my jail. So he's hoping I won't accidentally-on-purpose kill him if he says he's the brother of a leading citizen. I promise you, Roan, I've seen boys like Donovan pull this kind of sympathy stunt plenty of times."

Roan nodded. A leading citizen. With money and respect and supportive in-laws and a loving marriage. Donovan threatened everything he'd built for himself, for me, for us; everything he'd risked by coming back to Dunderry for my sake.

Alvin knocked on the door. "Tiffany, it's Sheriff Tobbler. Your mama says it's okay for you to open the door."

Slowly, the door cracked. A worried teenage face, chubby and acne-scarred, peered out. "I didn't do nothing wrong. I'm just babysittin'. The baby's got the shits, but she had 'em when he left her with me."

"We know. Let us in."

Tiffany's bewildered eyes scanned Roan and me. Roan's face made her gasp. Her eyes skittered back to me. "Mrs. Sullivan!"

"It's okay, Tiff."

"That guy promised to pay me when he got back. I been here five hours."

I pulled fifty dollars from my leather tote. "There. Will that do?"

"Shit, you pay good. Thanks, Mrs. Sullivan."

"Come by the newspaper office. Remember, you promised to write something for me."

"Yeah. I been working on some stories. But I'm a mama now, so I'm too busy."

She eased aside. She balanced a fat, grubby toddler on her hip as she pointed to the room's bed. "I changed her diapers and tried to feed her. She stinks but she's clean."

All I could see at the center of the dingy bed, among a nest of pink baby blankets with store tags still attached, was a small, beautiful, unhappy face. A soft wail came from the face's pale lips. I rushed over and pulled the swaddling of blankets aside. She wore a pink romper, stained with vomit. Her hair was soft black with a reddish tint, and fuzzy. Her skin was a deep gold color. She wasn't a newborn, but couldn't be more than six months old.

"Well, this is fascinating," Alvin said grimly. "Donovan has a high-yellow baby." If Alvin, a black man, wanted to describe her that way, that was his business. But all I saw was a fragile, beautiful little girl with big, gray, Sullivan eyes.

Yes, most babies have gray eyes in the first six months, and then their true color emerges. But these were *Sullivan* gray. I was convinced.

"Donovan's telling the truth," I said hoarsely. I slid my hands under her, cradled her to my sweater, and straightened. I rocked her, talked to her, and stroked her hair. When I turned to look at Roan and Alvin, I realized I'd missed a conversation between them. And another between Alvin and the office. Alvin had his cell phone to his ear. "Yeah. We'll wait." He snapped the phone shut. "EMT's will be here in a minute. They'll take over. And I've got a call into DFACs."

I scowled at him. "Why? We'll take her to the hospital ourselves. She's probably just got diarrhea. We'll have her checked out by a doctor and then take her home . . ."

My voice trailed off. I finally realized how Roan was staring at me. More precisely, at the baby. It was hard to decipher his expression among the lumps and stitches, but the look in his eyes froze my bones.

"She's not ours," he said. "We don't even know if Donovan's telling the truth. She's not coming home with us."

I held the baby closer. Her cries had quieted when I picked her up. She curled a soft hand against my throat. Motherhood is often unwarranted, careless, cherished, and all of the above.

I covered the back of her head with a protective hand. *She's already mine*, I thought. I looked at Roan in disbelief. "I gave Donovan my word. This is your *niece*."

"Now, Claire," Alvin said. "It'll take tests to prove that."

"Not to me. Look at her eyes, Roan."

"No. Stop it. Please." He was struggling. He wasn't a cruel person, he wasn't heartless. He certainly wasn't racist. It had nothing to do with skin color.

No, what he was, was a Sullivan. Big Roan's son.

Correction.

Big Roan's *first* son.

We were back on Steckem Road, and he hated the place. He'd worked too hard to get away from everything it represented. I understood. But . . . I tried again, in a hoarse, urgent whisper. "She's your *niece*, Roan. I feel it in my soul. Your niece."

He exhaled. I saw the grimace of his teeth, bloody from the wounds, polished by pain and the raw facts of survival. "If she is, then we'll find her a home," he said. "But not with us."

4

WHEN I MARRIED Roan, my family presented every one of our wedding gifts with a side dressing of sage advice. And so we were warned by my mother, daddy, grandmother, aunts, uncles, married cousins, and every relationship book ever published: *Marriage is about compromise, and the true test comes when neither of you will give in.*

"That's when you two will have to roll back your rugs and look hard at your foundation," Grandma Dottie told us. "Are you standing on the same rock, no matter what, or is that fine, dangerous crack you see going to grow wider and wider until it splits you apart?"

I spent most of the next week looking under our rugs. So did Roan. We tried to talk about Donovan and the baby but ended up saying nothing less painful. He dutifully gave a mouth swab for the DNA test. "It will show if you and Donovan share 'a common male ancestor,'" the hospital technician said. A polite description for the evil entity that had been Big Roan Sullivan. Donovan gave a swab at the jail. A pediatric nurse at the hospital gently took a smear from inside the baby's cheek. Such an intimate connection—three souls bound by sheer cotton on a stick.

"There's nothing to discuss until the tests come back," Roan said.

I couldn't leave at that. "And if they're positive?"

"Then Donovan signs custody over to us. He's going back to prison. He doesn't have a lot of options."

"And then?"

"And then you and I decide what to do with the baby."

"What should we decide to 'do' with your *niece*, other than adopt her?"

"Dammit. Think about it. A dead mother who abandoned her, a drug dealer and thief for a father, and dear ol' Grandpa Sullivan was . . ."

"So we'd give her away to strangers in order to let her start with a blank slate? Just so she'd never know . . . never be . . . *embarrassed* about her Sullivan family tree?" Bad choice of words. I winced. "Roan, I'm not trying to minimize—"

"It's my family tree," he said tightly. "And 'embarrassing' is an understatement for it."

"If that's how you feel, how can you and I have children of our own?"

"My God, Claire, that's different."

"How?"

"Because you'll be their mother, and *your* family will make up for my side of the deal. Your family wallows in bloodlines. That's the only reason they welcomed Matthew with open arms. That's why he fits in. Because he's one of them."

"Wallows in bloodlines," I echoed in a small voice. "You think that's all there is to the bond? You don't understand the meaning of 'family' at all."

"You're right. And maybe you expect too much from me if you think I'll ever believe some greeting-card ideal."

That hurt. And he knew it hurt.

This time he couldn't buy me a shamrock charm to change the subject.

So the baby was now firmly in the grasp of social services and would not be leaving the hospital anytime soon. Her ailments included dehydration, diarrhea, an ear infection and a cold. Visitors were forbidden.

I heard through my hospital sources (Rebecca and Violet, and Rebecca's boyfriend, Sonny, a nurse) that she cried endlessly. "Just colic," everyone said.

No. She needed me. She needed Roan. Maybe she even needed her biological father. Roan was so wrong about family bonds. Science might tell us we aren't related, but blood can be spiritual as well as physical.

Zach Donovan sat morosely in the Dunderry Jail, refusing to tell anyone even his little girl's name. He would only say that her mother was dead. He would not offer even a single word of explanation as to how two very opposite tracks had intersected at her birth.

He had loved—or at least slept with—a woman of color.

Then he'd joined a racist prison gang who hated women of color.

In the meantime, as word spread that the punk who'd ruined the festival might be Roan's half-brother, and the baby he claimed as his own might therefore be Roan's niece—of course, no one said 'the half-black baby,' but it was implied—the collective mood of Maloneys and Delaneys began to darken. They stewed the news as if boiling a tough shoulder of ham. They wanted to see which chunks fell off the bone first. I pictured my kin hunkered around those tender flecks of fallen meat like voodoo shamans, trying to read the patterns in it.

Where and how would Donovan and the baby fit in with us? Was it even possible?

"HUCK IT, CLAIRE! Huck it! Huck it, Claire, huck it!"

Huck is kayak talk for "run the waterfall." Fifty wet-suited and helmeted kids merrily chanted for me to plunge down a whitewater falls local kayakers called the Dipper Slipper. The Dipper Slipper was one of the Cheetowah's tamer runs by kayak standards, only a class two, but since the kids had already realized I wasn't much of a paddler, they hoped I'd flip over in the frigid March water. The Cheetowah River plunged over the Tennessee/Georgia state line on its way from the wintry Smokies down to their shorter, warmer sisters, our Cohuttas. Even on a sixty-degree spring day the water felt like liquid nitrogen.

"Huck the Dipper Slipper, Claire, come on!"

I wagged my paddle and peered nervously through my goggles at the tame pool of gray-green river water waiting twenty yards ahead. The devil of pride whispered in my ear. *Comeon, don't be a chickenshit, this is easy stuff. And Roan's watching you.*

Further downstream the Cheetowah roared through huge boulders down a long, steep series of class four and five rapids known as Jackjaw. Jackjaw was not for the faint of heart or wobbly of paddle. Roan, Matthew and a pre-pregnancy Tweet, all expert kayakers from their outdoorsy years in Alaska, routinely *hucked* that turbulent run, but I refused to try. I stood squeamishly on the banks, watching them each time, secretly terrified, ready to hurl a rescue rope if need be, along with my lunch.

Now Roan returned the favor, though he looked utterly calm. He towered among the kids and his fellow kayakers on the river banks, including Matthew and Tweet. Even though his face was a painful mess and he could barely flex his hands he'd insisted on doing our monthly volunteer work for the Cohutta Kayakers Club. The club brought city kids to the river and taught them the basics of water safety.

Roan lifted a hand to me then placed it gingerly over the heart of his black wetsuit. Gallant support. He wouldn't laugh if I turned over. In his condition, he couldn't even crack a smile.

Deep breath. *You can do this. Ignore your heritage.* Most Maloneys don't kayak. We don't even canoe. We are bass boat people. We sit on coolers of beer and bourbon with one hand on a fishing pole and the other on the WHAT of a good Evinrude trolling motor. If we fall in the water it's *never* intentional, and as we drag our khaki-butted behinds back into the boat we leave an oil slick of high-SPF sunscreen. In the family that's known as Irish Moisturizer.

But I was a Sullivan now. And Sullivans liked to huck a whitewater waterfall. So I checked my helmet's chin strap, patted the safety latches on my life vest, and took another deep breath.

"Eeee yah!" I yelled, thrust my paddle into the water, and launched myself into the toothless maw of the mild-mannered Dipper Slipper. The stereophonic rumble of whitewater drummed my ears. Cold white foam splattered my face below the goggles. Splash, turn, twist, scoot, victory!

I slid into the pool, right-side up, grinning. Everyone applauded. Roan couldn't, since his hands were so swollen, but he looked proud as he managed a thumbs up with the unsplinted hand.

Later, sitting on the riverbank watching Roan, Matthew and the others instruct the kids in a flotilla of kayaks in the calm safety of the river pool, Tweet grinned at me wickedly. "You are a total geek-sap for love."

I finished drying my long wet braid and arched a brow at her. "Dr. Sullivan, if you weren't pregnant I'd push you in the water."

"You hate kayaking. You should just tell Roan."

"Nope. This is one of his few real hobbies. Between the home restoration business and all his wheeling-dealing deals for land, he's always working."

"So do you. The newspaper and all. And you do so much with Roan."

"I love it. I love him."

"He wants to start an outfitter's business, you know. He's mentioned it to Matthew. He's serious."

"I know."

"Claire, if Donovan's baby turns out to be Roan's niece, are you sure you want to add that complication to your life?"

"She's family. You don't turn your back on family."

"I understand, but . . ."

"You think Roan and I aren't really ready to have children?"

"I know you are, but he never talks about wanting children. Are you sure *he's* ready?"

"No," I admitted, slumping. "I worry that he's humoring me."

"So . . . you go kayaking out of love for him, and he agrees to be a daddy out of love for you? Maybe he isn't ready to huck that waterfall, Claire."

"Maybe not. I don't know. I can't get him to talk about it. So, true to my nature, I'm just forging ahead."

A young voice pierced the crowd in the river. "But Mr. Sullivan, I *want* to roll upside down!"

Roan stood in the shallows, a handsome silhouette in the clinging wetsuit. The white gauze of his splinted finger made a strange contrast. He'd promised to let Matthew and the other adults do the heavy lifting today. He was in pain. "Trust me, pal," he called. "You don't want to learn how to roll over in water this cold. Keep that paddle level. Just practice bracing."

"I want to roll."

"I don't recommend it."

I'm gonna roll!"

The small adventurer lurched starboard. His head and torso disappeared in the dark water and his child-sized kayak flipped neatly upside down. We counted one, two, three as it *stayed* upside down. The water churned.

Roan dove, bareheaded, into the water, surfaced beside the kayak, grabbed its hull with his injured hands, and deftly righted NAME. Sputtering and dripping, NAME burst into tears. Steam rose off him. His teeth immediately began to chatter. "C-c-cold." He cried harder.

"You did fine," Roan told him. Now you're a real kayaker. You're tough."

Roan tugged him and his kayak into the shallows. Matthew slogged over with a blanket. As Matt unlatched the boy and pulled him out, Roan said, "When you're ready to try again, let me know. I won't let you drown."

The kid finally managed a smile.

I put a hand on Tweet's and leaned close to her. "You see that? You see that sweet man who isn't aloof or too quiet or just a bit cynical? That man who makes frightened children feel safe? That's the side of him that comes out around kids. They need him. And he needs them."

Tweet nodded her blonde head and gave me a wistful smile. "I see."

MAYBE ROAN WAS at least a *little* right about my family's fixation on blood ties. Each year, new group pictures updated our family photo albums. Every year, an annual accounting. A *State Of The Family Union* report, with photographic evidence. Because every year, the pictures starred a slightly different collection of faces.

The ones who didn't fit in, who had some beef that couldn't be resolved, some old bitterness that finally erupted, those faces vanished.

New ones, born or married, took their place. The loss-gain ratio was heavily weighted to "gain." Like a strict church preaching seductive fellowship and a happening social scene, we pick up more converts than we lose.

We ran Dunderry, both the town and the county. Us and our related families, including the Tobblers. We were benign dictators for the most part, keeping the peace and doling out justice as needed, like the mob running Las Vegas in the Rat Pack years. We forgave certain foibles, but not others. A lot depended on personal social skills and a willingness to remain part of the tribe. To compromise and acknowledge the general consensus.

If, for example, you dated a Jew, Hindu, Muslim or Mormon, (that list included a wide variety of unacceptable religious leanings, including psychics and faith healers, but those were the main culprits) you best keep it discreet and, for God's sake, don't marry one of them.

If you were gay or lesbian, move somewhere else, don't talk about it in front of the elderly, and come back, alone, for reunions. And, again, *don't marry one of them.*

If you were convicted of embezzlement or any other crime against paperwork, do your time, beg forgiveness in front of your church, and hire a better lawyer for the future.

If you were convicted of a crime of the flesh, and we knew for sure you did it, you were finished. Your name vanished from the family Bibles and your nearest kin decided somewhere else was a nice place to live. We didn't mention you again.

Zach Donovan, if bonafide, came very close to fitting that category.

Y'all need to take that baby away from him, he's a bad daddy, people told me with the best intentions, I'm sure. *Give it to good folks somewhere else. It'll grow up happy and decent. Just not here. Best for the baby, and best for us. Best for Roan. Poor man. He can't help what he comes from.*

My God. For the most part, everyone agreed with Roan. I began to wonder. Did they harbor a secret part of that 'best for' equation? Did they whisper? Should I worry?

We don't need any more Sullivan blood around here.

WE WAITED FOR DNA tests to come back from a lethargic, state-approved lab. In the meantime, various citizens began to realize they shared a peculiar problem of the automotive variety. Their catalytic converters had been stolen.

By Zach Donovan.

During the festival he'd helped himself to the highly re-sellable 'cat cons' on about two dozen vehicles parked in a field just outside town, which was used as overflow parking for Dunderry's many civic events. Roan explained the process to me in one of the rare times when we actually *talked* to one another without a sad chill between us.

"You slide under, you use a hacksaw or a portable torch. You cut the cat con off in a few minutes," he said. "Then take it to your friendly neighborhood chop shop and sell it. They buy the converters because of the platinum pellets inside."

He knew more about chop shops than he admitted to anyone but me. That business had been part of his desperate teenaged years, when he had no other way to support himself and Matthew.

Donovan had hidden the stolen converters in an old truck—which he'd *also* stolen. Alvin found the stolen truck behind a construction dumpster at the Kehoe Victorian on Pine Street, which Stuart Kehoe, our mayor, was restoring. There, Donovan had also helped himself to an air compressor, a tool belt, and the home's antique doorbell, which had been in the Kehoe clan for about a hundred years.

Now a line of converter-deprived cars and trucks waited for rehab in the graveled lot beside O'Brien Automotive Repairs. They included, unfortunately, my brother Brady's Mercedes, Uncle Cully's Lexus convertible (bought to impress his fellow dentists when he was elected head of the state dental society,) and his daughter Annabeth's Hummer, a gift from Uncle Cully when she graduated with Emory University with the first female dentistry degree in the history of the Delaney clan. Other victimized vehicles included a brand-new, apple-red Ford F-250 with the extended cab, sporting a magnetic sign for Tobbler Apple Products, owned by Alvin's sister, Tula.

In my family, this was sacrilege. On the list of stuff we cherish, *Things On Wheels* rank in the top five along with God, Spouse, Kids, and Family.

And not necessarily in that order.

So Donovan could now add even more people to his list of enemies, which already included Alvin, all the other Tobblers and assorted other black citizens of Dunderry, plus Roan, of course, and the entire congregation of Mt. Gilead Methodist Church.

Mama, Daddy and my brothers wisely kept quiet about the consequences and their opinions of the outcome. Their silence worried me more than anything else.

MAMA ANGRILY dug a wide steel comb deeper into the shaggy fur of a tall, placid, mama llama Daddy had named Raquel Welch. Something about her big eyes and long legs, Daddy claimed. He sheared the llamas about once a year; in-between, Mama collected llama wool by brush. It was a soothing chore, for both people and beasties. Amanda and I often helped comb the critters.

"You think I'd ever say a bad word about Roan or his people?" she asked hotly. She clutched the comb with both hands and rake it through Raquel's white fur. "You think I wouldn't be kind to that baby if y'all decided to keep it?"

"Mama, chill out. I'm not accusing you. I'm just asking you to be honest with me. Mama! Chill! If you keep using the comb that way, Raquel's going to be bald."

She halted. "Oh, Miss Welch, Claire's right. I'm so sorry." She patted the llama's long, vertical neck. "Don't tell Holt I was too rough on you." Raquel, her furry ears swiveling over her dour llama face, eyed Mama as if Mama might deserve a wad of llama spit. The llama herd adored Daddy. Not so much, the rest of us.

Mama's cell phone buzzed. She talked furiously into thin air, the cord of her ear bud bouncing like an electrified snake. "No, I do not know, Jane. Yes, it might be very soon. Or it might be another week. *I will call you later.*"

Click

"Let me guess," I said. "Everyone's asking about those test results."

"Nothing wrong with curiosity."

"Mama, is this family ready to accept a mixed-race baby?"

She sagged. "Some are. Some aren't. Most would keep their mouths shut, either way. Or your daddy and I would skin 'em alive."

"What if Josh had married Lin Su?" My brother dated a Vietnamese-American woman for several years. They were practically engaged when, suddenly, he met Karen. Amanda and I, among others, hadn't forgiven Josh for dumping Lin Su.

"I liked Lin Su a whole lot better than I like prissy-butt Karen."

"But Karen's a better political choice."

"Baby, I don't know if your brother looked at it that way, or not." My mother tugged wads of soft llama fur off the comb and threw it a tall laundry hamper with WOOL STORAGE written on its plastic side in black marker. Several of her Delaney cousins had taken up heritage crafts that included spinning and dyeing their own yarn; they toured the craft show circuit selling llama yarn to upscale knitters, including me. Several of Raquel Welch's fellow llamas stood near me, sniffing at my lopsided llama-wool sweater as if I might be a secret member of their herd.

"How do *you* look at it, Mama? At this baby."

She sighed. "It's not the baby. It's the daddy. What if he's a hanger-on? He'll get out of prison eventually and probably head straight back to you and Roan looking for money. You and Roan could end up having to *bribe* him to leave you and his daughter alone. He could very well make your life and that little girl's life miserable as long as he lives."

She was right.

I stared dully out the barn's big double doors. Springtime was not shaping up to be a happy season for us, and I had been looking forward to it so much. The mountains were about to bloom with infinite shades of green. I could hear toads clucking wildly as they turned Grandma Dottie's big, ornamental goldfish pond into a splashing, churning, toad-pool orgy. Llamas, horses and beef cattle grazed together in big pastures.

The farm's main house looked so pretty in the sunshine. Big and sprawling, it showed its pedigree on its multi-peaked roof line—two elderly stone chimneys from the 1830's, three modern brick chimneys from the 1950's, and three satellite dishes from the 1990's. In the flower beds of the back yard, siblings of the Dunshinnog foxgloves angled their spring spires toward the sky. They'd bloom by May or June. In the meantime, butter-yellow jonquils were popping up everywhere.

Easter was coming in a couple of weeks. Renewal. Rebirth. Chocolate bunnies. What a beautiful world. I had loved growing up here. And Roan loved the place too, after he came to live with us. His niece—or even if she turned out *not* to be his niece—should grow up here as we had. Playing here, being part of this big, quirky but ultimately loving family and this wonderful place, where the foxgloves bloomed.

I picked up a brush and went to work on the nearest llama. I needed the therapy.

"I'M THINKING about applying to be a foster mother for the Donovan baby," Tula announced at her apple-scented shop in town, Tobbler Apple Goods. I was so surprised I just stared at her. She held up a package of Tobbler Apple Fritters and a jar of Tobbler Fine Apple Relish, frowned, then tucked them among the foam peanuts inside a small shipping box. Every month Tula sent a gift of Tobbler

Apple Goods to Oprah Winfrey's offices up in Chicago. Tula included a full-color Tobbler Apple Goods catalog and a pitch letter outlining why Oprah should give a sister a break and feature her on the show. So far, Oprah's staff hadn't even bothered to send a thank-you note for the tasty food. But Tula wouldn't stop trying. Tobblers didn't surrender.

I stuck a Tobbler Mini-Cobbler in the bribe box. "You and Charley have three small children of your own. Why would you want to take on a baby?"

"There aren't that many black families in the county."

"Who says the foster family has to be black?"

"It's a black baby."

"She's half-white."

"In this world, that means she's black. She needs to be with people who look like her."

"She has gray eyes."

"So? My grandpa had *blue* eyes and freckles, thanks to you-know-who. That didn't stop the police from hosing him when he marched with Dr. King in Alabama."

"No need to bring our great-grandpa Liam into this."

"Claire, a whole lot has changed for the better, but a whole lot hasn't changed, too. People still care about the differences."

"Zach Donovan was trying to take care of his child. You have to give him credit for that much."

"Why are you defending that Nazi yokel? Is *Roan* feeling that charitable? I bet not. I saw him this morning. His face is still such a shiny shade of blue and purple."

I scowled. "I thought you and I agreed to announce our cousinhood at the millennium. And that means putting aside racial politics."

Tula shook a jar of Tobbler Apple-Cinnamon Sugar-Free Apple Butter at me. "Zach Donovan called my brother a *nigger*. That baby of his needs to be raised by people of color who'll teach her right from wrong."

"I agree. But they could be *white* people of color."

"Oh, no you don't, Claire. Don't you bat those eyes at me and give me that can't-we-all-just-get-along look. You're a bleeding-heart Democrat." She hugged me but then pulled back and arched a black brow beneath a glossy swoop of straightened, no-nonsense hair. Tobblers had gone Republican along with the rest of the old-school Dunderry families. Their politics were a complex mix of tradition, pride, and practical ambition. "I love you anyway," Tula said wryly. "You damned liberal."

"I love you too, Miss Tula, you cold-hearted conservative. But . . ."

A gaggle of women entered the shop. Probably from Atlanta, out for a day of rustic hillbilly tours. All white, all well-heeled. Tula and I rolled our eyes at each other over a sea of pashmina scarves and embroidered hip jackets. One of the women turned to me, smiling her lip-lined smile. "Are you the shop's owner?"

They just assumed the white girl was the owner. I nodded at Tula, who stood beneath some pretty obvious evidence that the shop was hers. On the wall directly behind her hung a large portrait in an ornate frame. The portrait showed a stern, unsmiling black couple, she in stiff black muslin and he in a stiff black suit, their hands resting proudly on the heavy wooden wheel of their apple press.

The portrait had been made from a scratched tintype of Addie and Barnabas Tobbler. They were respected figures now, but they didn't start out that way. They probably murdered their owner, a medicinal-rum peddler named Houck, in 1840, when they arrived with him to the log-cabin splendor of downtown Dunderry.

All anyone knew for sure was that Houck left behind nothing but a puddle of blood and a scrap of his blond scalp, that a Delaney bought his wagon and a Maloney bought his rum, and the Tobblers used the cash from those sales to buy their homestead and start an apple orchard. And thus are history and family and communal loyalty made. On shared fruit and murder, need and service and secrets.

Tula arched a brow at me as the white women continued to look at *me* for assistance. "I told you so," she mouthed.

"This lovely lady's the shop owner," I ordered them, nodding at Tula. "I know it's confusing. We do look alike. We're kin."

The women blushed and made small talk to hide their confusion. Tula picked up a fresh apple from a large metal tray on the shop's candy counter. The apple, a Tobbler Dipped Deluxe, was covered in zebra swirls of white and dark chocolate. Ignoring the irony, Tula threatened to throw it at me.

I left the building.

"YOU DIDN'T GET this from *me*," Freddie Delaney whispered at tryouts for the Dunderry Girls Twelve-and-Up softball team. I sat in the bleachers at the community ball fields, coaching Amanda. She had an arm like John Smoltz but we'd been working on her erratic swing. This was her first year in the Twelve-Up League, an exciting step forward. Plus the league had picked up *Chic-fil-A* as a sponsor, thanks to our cousin Sheila Maloney Pittman and her husband, who owned four franchises in north Georgia alone. There'd be plenty of free chicken nuggets at every game.

I stared at the folded softball schedule Freddie slapped on the knee of my jeans. He strolled on past, nodding to the coaches and little girls as if there was nothing odd about a sudden need for armed patrols of the dugouts.

What was this, an early April Fool's joke? I opened the brochure. Inside, Zach Donovan had scrawled a plea on a torn sheet of notepad paper.

To Clar Sullivan. Im worreed about my babi. Can u chek on her? She dont dserv to be lonelee.

I folded the sad note and slipped in a pocket of my sweater. I shivered. Cool spring sunshine spilled gentle afternoon shadows across the well-kept softball fields, the nice bleachers and concession stands. Everywhere I looked I saw smiling adults, healthy children, comfort, leisure and prosperity.

Zach Donovan understood the threat to his daughter. He knew how easy it is for good people to forget about a child like his.

"I COULD LOSE my job over this," Sonny Cole said. "But what's a job when my baby-loving conscience is at stake? Besides, when I act like an outlaw, Rebecca thinks I'm sexier."

Sonny was a pediatric nurse at the hospital. He and Rebecca had begun dating a few months after she divorced her husband for cheating on her. She required a tricky mix of sensitivity and Alpha male pecker waggling. Sonny could handle the pressure. As a student at Auburn he'd played Aubie, the university's famous tiger mascot. At football games, Aubie routinely risked getting the polyester stuffing beaten out of him by rival University of Alabama fans.

"This won't take long," Roan assured him.

"You have five minutes. After that, I won't have any idea how you two slipped into the pediatrics ward at midnight. Security's tight. Poor kid."

"Claire'll hurry."

I turned to Roan, who was gazing grimly down the hospital's empty midnight hallway. "Are you sure you don't want to see her?"

"Yes."

"All right. I'll be back in a few minutes."

Sonny pointed me toward an empty room, and laid a finger to his lips. I slipped inside. I looked down into a perfunctory, institutional crib.

She was asleep.

Here was a stranger's child who might share part of Roan's heritage. She was alone in the world right now, the subject of debate, her name unknown, her future uncertain. In Irish folklore there are tales about fairies stealing human babies and leaving their own rejected children in the babies' place. The stories, cruel in their practicality, were used to explain sick or disabled kids. Those must be the outcast children of evil fairies.

I looked down at Donovan's little girl and fell in love again. This time, the fairies had left one of their princesses by mistake.

THE DUNDERRY County Jail had changed a lot since Roan and I were kids. In the old days, Big Roan slept off his violent binges in a cell with plaid curtains on the window bars. The jail occupied a friendly brick building just off the square. The path from Maloney Elementary to the town baseball field went right past the back doors. We kids would wave at the inmates, and they waved back. The sheriff's wife grew zinnias and tomatoes in a side garden. There were no fences. The bolder inmates occasionally swiped the cell keys and let themselves out for a walk. Most came back voluntarily.

Now the jail was known as the Dunderry County Correctional Facility. It squatted in sinister, institutional splendor on five scalped acres well outside town, surrounded by a wall of chain link and rolled barbed wire. The scraped land next door bore a large sign that warned:

FUTURE SITE OF THE DUNDERRY COUNTY WASTE TREATMENT PLANT

In the old days we'd had a plain old county dump. Now we needed waste treatment. Our garbage and our inmates had become big business.

I sat down on my side of a plexiglass wall and thumped a finger on the little built-in speaker that Zach and I would have to use for communicating. "Testing. Testing."

"That thump hurt my ear drum," Freddie said over an intercom.

I waved at a one-way window overlooking the room. "Sorry."

"What's in the basket?"

"A care package for Donovan. Alvin cleared it. I'll leave it at the front desk."

"Does Roan know you're here?"

I thumped the speaker again. Freddie yelped.

A steel door opened on the other side of the see-through wall. Deputy Arnie Kehoe guided the handcuffed Zach into the room, pointed to the chair facing mine, waited sternly until Zach was seated, then scowled at me.

"Thanks, cousin," I said.

He shook his head and shut the steel door hard behind him on the way out. News of my jail visit would spread faster than ice cream melts on a July sidewalk.

Zach Donovan stared at me from under his bruised eyelids, and I stared back. He still looked fairly awful. The up-glow off an orange jumpsuit didn't do much for his freckled complexion, especially when his face was still covered in puffy knots turning a glossy shade of bluish-purple. I cleared my throat. "I'm happy to see that your face still looks worse than my husband's."

He worked his swollen mouth. Then, slowly, "Is there . . . anybody in this . . . town who ain't . . . married to you or blood kin to you?"

I shook my head. "I think you're about the only one."

He leaned forward. "How's my baby?"

"She's good. I've seen her. She's beautiful. Healthy."

"People hate her 'cause of me?"

"No."

"'Cause she's mixed?"

"No."

"Liar."

I squinted a warning. "*They don't hate her*. Let's change the subject. Why won't you tell us her name?"

"Because y'all will just go ahead and name her whatever you like anyhow. But I'm the only one who knows what her *real* name is. It's all I've got."

"No one's saying you'll lose your rights as her father."

He smiled thinly. The flash of teeth, the wolfish lilt to it. I leaned forward, fixated. It was Roan's smile.

"I ain't stupid," he was saying. "I'm going back to prison for quite a spell. I ain't gonna get no chance to be her daddy."

"Tell me the truth about one thing. How can you love your daughter if you hate black people?"

He seethed. "I don't . . . hate nobody. I just use whatever weapon I can best use against anybody who gets in my face."

"Oh. So . . . you're a *circumstantial* bigot. For example, you don't hate women, but if I made you spectacularly angry, would you fight back by calling me oh, say, a bitch or a cunt?"

We heard a loud rattle and thump over the intercom. Donovan looked up at the window warily. I tapped on the plexiglass to regain his attention. "It's just cousin Freddie falling off his chair. Answer my question. Do you use racist language as a weapon when it's the only way you can hit back?"

His big shoulders sagged a little. "Yeah." Then he squared his jaw. "But I ain't never called a woman those names. White, black, yellow, green, purple. No color of woman. Never."

"Good."

"What are you gettin' at?"

"That you're not a racist, you just play one on TV."

"What the—"

"It's a joke."

"Your jokes make me nervous."

"Will you at least tell me more about the baby's mother?"

"She handed the baby over to a girlfriend and split before I come home from prison. Took up with somebody else." He looked away. His jaw worked. "She loved a bad dude. Lots worse than me. Got herself killed."

"She didn't love you but you loved *her*."

His fierce attention came back to me. "That ain't none of your business."

"Did she leave you for a black guy?"

"Look, I didn't ask you to come here and grill me about my life. I just wanted to hear how my kid is."

"Why? You've given her away. Why do you care how she is?"

He straightened ominously. "I don't . . . I can't . . ." His bleak eyes bored into me. "Don't you play games with me. This ain't about me. It's about *him*. He doesn't want her, does he? Your husband. My . . . he don't believe me. And even if them tests prove I ain't lying, he *still* doesn't want to believe me. He doesn't want to take care of her for me."

"He wants what's best for her. Don't you?"

"That's why I brought her here. I heard how he was raised. My ol' mama talked about him. She said you helped him when y'all were kids. She said he turned out fine. She said he'd help me, and so would you. So much for that."

"He does care. But he doesn't know if he can trust you."

"*'Course* he can't trust me." Donovan laughed bitterly. "I'm a tattooed convict."

"What would you do if he dropped the charges? Be honest."

Zach Donovan thought for a moment, started to speak, frowned, then shook his head. "I don't know."

"You better make up your mind then. Think about what your daughter is worth to you. And whether or not you have what it takes to *earn* the right to be her father."

"What's that mean?"

"Like you said, 'I don't know,' yet."

"Time's up," Freddie said over the intercom.

I stood. I gestured at the basket. "Candy bars, peanuts, chewing gum, and some magazines. I thought about bringing you a Bible and a biography of Rosa Parks, but I relented and brought you some issues of Playboy, instead. It's the thinking man's pornography. Can you read better than you write?"

"Of course I can . . ." he halted. "What do you want from me?"

"I made you a promise to help your daughter. You're not making it easy to keep that promise. Why?"

"I'm done here. Nothing else to say. You . . . I don't know what to make of you but . . . don't come back to see me. I ain't gonna talk to you again." He stood and looked up at the window. A tiny, wicked smile managed to find a home on his battered lips. "Hey, cousin Freddie! Tell cousin Arnie to come get me, you hear?"

I had to admire his style. "I'll leave the basket up front. Cousin Arnie will make sure you get it. By the way, I lied about the *Playboys.* I brought you copies of *Parenting Today* and *American Baby.*"

"Why? You're just gonna give my daughter to some strangers to raise."

Stalemate. I gave him my patented blue-eyed stare, hoping he'd break. He merely scowled at me until Arnie entered the room. I exhaled in defeat and turned to go.

"Hey," Donovan said quietly. "I mean . . . hey, ma'am."

I looked back. Ma'am? I was only ten years older than he. "Yes, *sir*?"

He pursed his lips in deep concentration as Arnie latched a beefy hand on his arm. "Thank you." he finally managed. "Thank you for giving a shit."

Arnie growled at his language and jerked him hard.

My heart twisted. "You're welcome."

His shoulders sagged. "Her . . . her name is . . . *Forsythia.*"

No wonder he'd kept it secret. Good lord. I lied. "That's a beautiful name."

"Her mama didn't bother naming her. I did. I just . . . I like that tough ol' bush. The flowers. They're a pretty yellow. They come back every spring."

"Thank you for telling me."

We'd made at least a little progress. Proper etiquette, albeit with a little shit on top, is always a good sign.

Two days. The results were promised within two days.

Our home, our sanctuary up on Dunshinnog, simmered with a tension I'd never thought possible. Even our big bed of heirloom foxgloves looked worried, sending up timid green shoots from the soft mounds of green that had survived the winter. I sat there every afternoon on a bench we'd installed, waiting for Roan to come up from town, looking out over the Estatoe Valley, then looking back at our house.

We were so proud of it. It was unique. A half-cave. During the months when we were digging and burrowing and building into the mountain side, pretty much every citizen of Dunderry County—all five thousand two hundred and change—found some excuse to drop by and take a look. Compliments warred with open-jawed stares. I knew some of my younger kin were thinking: *They're going to grow weed up here, we bet.*

The front rooms made a handsome denture of log and stone, smiling discreetly from the mountain's western face. The view of sunsets was incredible. The cave-home's free-thinking design summed up how we saw ourselves together and how we saw the community beyond and below us.

The back bed rooms were *inside* the mountain. Their walls included mountain bedrock. Sunlight and moonlight that poured down through large solar panels set in the mountain stone above our heads. On warm nights Roan and I lay in bed naked, looking up at the sky. The front rooms and veranda protruded out over the mountain's bouldered ridge above a descending panorama of woods and rocky ledges. People loved to sit there. Good. I had slowly accustomed Roan to a comfortable schedule in which he hosted human beings other than myself. Matthew and Tweet came up to our home every Wednesday for dinner.

"Talk to him, Matthew," I urged.

Matthew, clean-cut, comfortable in his own skin, and, thanks to Roan, unencumbered by bitter childhood experiences that might color his perspective, launched into a cheerful lecture over a grilled steak dinner on our stone patio. It probably didn't help that Roan's recovery had not yet reached a point where he could chew beef.

"Bigger, you've got to lighten up," Matthew said breezily. "You know, I'm a Sullivan, too. Maybe in name only but I'm proud of it.

This Donovan, if he's . . . one of us, then . . . maybe we can *help* him. The way Claire helped you, and you helped me."

Roan set aside his cup of mashed potatoes with beef gravy. Then, speaking very softly, always a bad sign, he said, "Let's get something straight. I never did prison time, I never tried to rob anybody at gunpoint, I never joined a racist gang, and when you were a kid, *I never risked losing you.*"

And that was the end of that conversation.

I GOT OUT of bed and went to the veranda that night, wrapped in a weirdly off-kilter shawl I'd knitted. I curled up on a lounge chair for no more than ten minutes before Roan followed me. We sat there in the dark, the silence growing sadder and deeper. "I want my best friend back," he said gruffly.

"So do I," I whispered.

He held out a hand, still bruised and swollen. It made me cry, and we went back to bed.

THE CALL ABOUT the lab results came from Alvin on a Saturday evening, of all times. He left the news on our kitchen answering machine.

I taped it on a mini-recorder I used for interviews at the newspaper, then stuck the tape player in my robe's pocket. A herd of cats and dogs followed me as I made my way through the house and onto the deep, screened veranda. I carried a mug of hot tea medicated with two shots of bourbon. I wore a thick terrycloth robe, a long UGA sweatshirt, flipflops and nothing else.

Outside, a crisp, starry sky capped the Estatoe Valley below us. Until the trees leafed out I could glimpse the friendly wink of lights from Mama and Daddy's place. I picked my way down stone steps that wound through wild laurel and huckleberry.

I heard a rustling sound above the house. I looked up, expecting to see the dark silhouettes of deer looking back at me. No deer. Just the wind, then. Or a raccoon heading for our bird feeders. Maybe even a young black bear. Or my nerves.

This was before I heard Mercy Honey on the mountain. I shivered and hurried down the remaining stairs. Roan sat naked in our inventive version of a hot tub with his head back on a pillow, a large ice pack on his still-healing face, and his eyes shut. Steam rose around him. We'd built the hot tub into a cluster of rocks a dozen yards below our equally odd home.

I sat down next to him and lowered my bare legs into the steaming water. I gently removed the ice pack. "Hello." He eased his head up. I held a straw to his lips. "Here. Sip this. Good for what ails you."

He drew from it gingerly, took the mug, and set it aside. "You talked to Alvin?"

"How did you—"

"I saw him in town this morning. He told me he'd probably call with the DNA results today. I can tell by the look on your face."

"There's a message." I pulled the tape player from my robe. "Ready?"

"No." I laid the player on my lap. We looked at the moonlit shadows rising in the hollows and the ripples of the mountains below us. Roan shook his head. "All right, Peep. Before we go any further, tell me what you really want to do if the DNA is a match. Then what? I love you and I'll go with your decision. But be as honest with me as you know how. Be honest with yourself."

"Honestly? I . . . want to *steal* the baby." My voice rose. "I want Donovan to just go away." I stared straight ahead. I could feel Roan's surprised gaze on me. "I'm not proud of that emotion, but hell, it's the truth. He's hauling a lot of baggage. I really don't get the feeling he's mean or vicious, just sort of *lost*, but his drifting moral compass could get a lot more people hurt. So I'd like to say some magic words and make him *vanish*. For the baby's sake. And for yours. So that you and I can be happy here, with the baby, without any ghosts from the past."

Roan laid his hand—the splint had just been removed from the broken finger—on my bare knee. "Now you understand how I feel."

I put my hand over his, turned the healing fingers, and traced the edge of a bruise that bisected his palm at the lifeline. "But I have to do what's right." I chuckled darkly. "My moral compass only points one way on this issue. Dammit."

"I already don't like the sound of that. Just when I thought it was safe to relax."

"If the DNA test confirms that Zach's the baby's father and that you and Zach are brothers—"

"Half-brothers. I'd like to keep saying it that way."

"Half-brothers. If that's true, then . . ." It was hard to get the words out. In my windpipe, that chimney of my soul, self-interest would always try to ambush true grace. "Then we have to give Zach Donovan a chance to become a good father."

I squinted in case Roan's reaction was very bad. A good squint reduces bad news to a manageable trickle. But when I looked at him, he was studying me with a sad smile. "I knew it would come to this. That you'd want to help him."

"Why?"

"Because you think he's *me*. If you can rescue him, you can rescue me, again. But don't make this about me, Peep. I'm ninety percent home."

I lifted Roan's palm to my lips. "I want to bring that last ten percent home, too."

"You're greedy."

"No, stubborn. I refuse to give up on achieving full 'homeness' for you. Full 'familyness,' too."

He nodded at the tape player. "Give me the news."

I clicked a control. Alvin's deep voice curled out.

"Congratulations, folks," he said grimly. "You've got yourself a couple of new Sullivans."

5

WHEN I WAS a little girl, my aunt Arnetta, who worked as Dunderry County's home extension agent, taught Sunday School the same humorless way she taught 4-H'ers to can tomatoes and disinfect baby bottles: as if sin were a germ she could kill with heat and bleach. This was long before I got in trouble with her for writing a poem praising Roanie Sullivan's *cajones*, a term I'd read in one of Daddy's forbidden paperback westerns and mistakenly defined as a non-testicular attribute.

". . . and so Cain wasn't much of a farmer, *was* he?" Aunt Arnetta lectured to us seven year olds. "He offered God an untidy, unscrubbed sacrifice of over-ripe produce, and God said, 'That's not up to proper preparation standards, Cain.' But God *praised* the nicely de-boned and marinated lamb that Cain's baby brother Abel had butchered for Him.

"Well! Jealousy and anger just ate Cain up. After all, he was the oldest brother, and he didn't think much of his baby brother putting on airs and getting lots of back-patting from God, even though Abel clearly deserved it.

"God *saw* that Cain was jealous of Abel, and God said to Cain, 'Now, see here, mister, just because you're the eldest son doesn't mean you can get by with offering me a bushel of rotten vegetables. Don't be mad at your brother for your own home economic failings. Look me in the eye, mister, and say you're sorry.'"

"But Cain was stubborn and proud. He saw his baby brother as putting on airs, like I said. He didn't think Abel was worthy of God's praise. So Cain lured Abel out into a cornfield, and in a moment of thoughtless anger, HE HIT HIM WITH A HOE AND KILLED HIM.

"Well! After awhile, God noticed that Abel hadn't come back to their farmhouse. He said, 'Cain, where's your baby bubba? Is he okay?' Cain shuffled his work boots for a minute, because he knew he was in hot water with God, then he kind of shrugged and answered like he still had a chip on his shoulder. 'How should I know? You expect me to be my brother's keeper?'

"*Well.* When God figured out Cain had slewn Abel with the hoe, God was very disappointed in Cain. Because God *did* expect him to be his brother's keeper. God expects ALL of us to be our brothers' keepers."

I could shut my eyes and still picture Aunt Arnetta speaking that last sentence in a high, trilling drawl. She towered above our class in a purple polyester dress with an empire waist and a mandarin collar. She looked awesome, hefty and regal. She was only in her forties, then, a dynamo of repressed sexual power. Her husband, Daddy's baby brother Eugene, seemed scared of her.

Maybe it was her hair. She curled her shoulder-length brown mane into stylish Farrah Fawcett flip-backed waves, but the flips never stayed in place; instead they slowly unfurled on either side of her face, splaying out from her jaws in symmetrical brown scoops that waggled every time she moved her head, like the horns of a water buffalo.

I was hypnotized.

"Who can tell me what the story of Cain and Abel means?" Aunt Arnetta asked the class. Her sharp eyes went straight to my glassy ones. She didn't approve of me, even then. I had a reputation for taking up for with white trash Roanie Sullivan. I'd already embarrassed my family more than once, on his behalf. "Claire?"

Clearly, she picked me because I had four brothers and a history of hitting them, though I'd never gone after one with a hoe. As I twiddled my long red hair and stared thoughtfully at the magnolia appliqué on my skirt, Aunt Arnetta repeated sternly, "Claire Maloney. Look at me. What do we learn from the story of Cain and Abel?"

Ahah. I had it. I looked up. "That you can't trust your brothers? And . . . you should hide their dead bodies quicker, so God won't find out?"

That, of course, was not the correct answer. Cain and Abel are a study in ritual versus faith. God suspected Cain was just going through the motions, worship-wise, while Abel exhibited a true calling. God warned Cain to straighten up, but Cain didn't get the point. So Cain killed Abel in a fit of 'Take *that*, you show-off,' and then God sentenced Cain to wander in a spiritual wilderness the rest of his life.

I didn't see Roan as a conniving Cain or Zach as an innocent Abel, but I worried that my doubting husband, who had good reason to fear and hate anything and anyone who dragged him back to the past, would only go through the motions of becoming his brother's keeper. If Roan couldn't develop at least a dollop of true faith in Zach, then Zach might end up lost to the grace of God, family and home, and Roan might end up lost, too.

Aunt Arnetta's Home Ec 101 version of the Cain and Abel tragedy played through my mind when Roan and Zach held their first official face-to-face as brothers.

The way it turned out, I was very glad neither one of them had access to a hoe.

THE SUNDAY morning after Alvin's call, while the rest of Dunderry whispered the DNA news across church pews, Roan and I walked into a small room at the jail and sat down at a small metal table. "Hi, Freddie," I said to the one-way window high on the wall.

"Hi, y'all," Freddie said over the intercom. "Happy Sunday-before-Palm-Sunday. Me and my band are playing gospel bluegrass for Dunderry First Baptist's Passion Week Concert."

"You should sneak in some 'Rocky Top' or 'Orange Blossom Special,'" I said to the window. "See if you can trick a few Baptists into dancing."

Freddie chortled.

Roan laid a handsome leather notebook on the table; I'd given it to him for a birthday, with his monogram in small bronze embossing in the lower right corner. Since his downtrodden mother, Jenny Bolton, never suggested a middle name, and Big Roan didn't care one way or the other, Roan's monogram was a simple RS. He was missing more than a symbolic piece of himself.

He flipped the notebook open and removed two identical sets of paperwork, each stapled firmly at the tops. He laid one set on the empty spot across from him, where Zach would sit. The other set he straightened methodically in front of himself.

I watched as his big, bruised hands gracefully aligned the paper, the setting, his thoughts, his demands. In the shower that morning he'd reached around me and gingerly cupped my naked breasts, a favorite hobby we'd had to forego in the past two weeks. I loved to look at his hands on me, and my hands on him.

The swelling in his left hand had gone down enough that he could once again wear his wide wedding band, a match for mine in unembellished gold. Now he pulled a heavy gold fountain pen—another gift from me—from an inner pocket of his soft leather aviator jacket. He hated suits and ties. Leather, khakis and black knit pullovers were his Sunday best. I couldn't coax him into any local church, but if I ever did he would fit in best with the Reverend Aunt Dockey Maloney's laid back Unitarian-Universalist congregation. Unitarian-Universalists are, after all, the tie-dyed t-shirts of the Protestant fashion catalog.

I looked down at my pink dress suit. Barbie doll stuff, not my usual post-hippy denim and fuzzy fiber. I'd decided a young-matron attitude might inspire Zach. He could picture himself as Ken's younger brother?

Roan laid the ink pen precisely parallel with his paperwork's left edge. Then he spread his large, healing hands on the metal table top and stared grimly at the bolted metal door across from us. Waiting.

"A Chinese rat," I teased in a whisper, leaning close to him so Freddie couldn't overhear. "You fit the profile perfectly."

He swiveled his frown to me. "A what?"

"That's your sign in Chinese astrology. The rat. Relentless and detail-oriented."

"You really know how to flatter a man."

No, but I knew how to distract one. "It's not a negative description. Rats are also charming, inventive and devoted to the people they trust."

"And the bad news is?"

"The people rats trust comprise a *very* small group. Rats are too suspicious."

"No, rats are smart." His eyes lightened just a bit. "All right, I'll bite. Or gnaw. Whatever. What sign are you in Chinese astrology?"

"A snake. Organized, intuitive, and kind." I lowered my voice to a dramatic purr. "And I can do amazing things with my forked tongue."

"Talking dirty to men in jail will get you in trouble. Save that thought." He focused intently on the door again. "Where the hell is he? Brushing his teeth and straightening his orange jumpsuit so he'll make a good impression at the family reunion?"

I sat back in a hard metal chair. "Let's give him this along with your lecture." I pulled some photos from my pink purse. "He'll like having pictures of Forsythia."

"He needs a baby naming book."

"Maybe we can suggest a nickname."

"What? 'For?' Or maybe 'Syth?' That has a nice ring. 'Syth Sullivan.' Jesus."

"Not 'Syth.' Everyone will think we have a lisp."

The door opened with a metallic *clank*. Arnie guided Zach into the small room, pointed at the chair on his side of the table and grunted, "Sit. Hands in lap. Stay."

"Bow wow," Zach drawled. It would have been funny except for the smirk on his face and the acid sarcasm in his voice. He slumped into the chair with a jingle of his handcuffs, splayed his long legs under the table, and set his attitude on full resistance. He glared at Roan. His buzz-cut hair had grown out enough to form a glossy, dark-brown cap.

His face was beginning to emerge from its bruises. Smooth-faced and a good fifty pounds leaner than his older brother, he suddenly bore a passing resemblance to the college student he might have become.

He was young enough to falter under Roan's steely, mature gaze. His eyes shifted to me for reprieve. Gray eyes. I confirmed them finally. Sullivan gray. He ducked his head in greeting. "You look good in pink."

Bad mojo, instantly. Roan shifted forward in his chair. That small warning got Zach's instant attention. "Keep your eyes on me," Roan warned softly. The subtext was clear: *Keep your eyes off my wife.*

I clamped a hand on Roan's forearm. "Thanks, Zach. But enough about me. We brought you some photos of Forsythia." I placed the pictures close to him on the table because he wasn't allowed to pick them up. The photos of his sleeping daughter made a stark contrast to the stern paperwork Roan pushed closer to the table's edge.

Zach stared at the photos. His throat worked. Suddenly his hands came from under the table. The cuffs rattled wildly as he scooped the photos up then tucked them inside the collar of his orange jumpsuit.

Freddie yelped over the intercom, "Donovan, if you put your hands on the table again without permission you're outta here."

Zach boiled over. "I'm gonna be outta here in a minute anyhow, cousin Freddie." His defiant went back to Roan. "Cause I doubt I'm gonna be interested in *anything* my big brother's about to say." Zach leaned forward, smiling a deadly wolf smile. "Howdy, *big brother.* Nice to meet you. Don't we favor one another? I hear we get our gray eyes from our old man. You don't look so happy to know we're blood kin. Do I look like our old man? I've never seen a picture of him. Mama said he had black hair. More like you than me. She said *you* never gave him a chance to be a good daddy to you. She said he wasn't too bad except when he was drunk."

Oh, God. What was Zach up to? *Easy, now, stay calm.* Zach used words as weapons. They were all he had. I could believe Daisy McClendon had told him some deluded version of the truth, but I could also believe Zach was making these jibes up to provoke Roan. Either way, it was working. I dug my fingers into Roan's arm. The muscles quivered.

Roan never took his eyes off his reckless baby brother. "Your mother was a liar." Roan's voice became a soft, lethal drawl. "Our old man was a worthless piece of shit. *And you remind me of him.*"

Zach's smile faded. He leaned closer, hunching over the table like a mad, wounded dog. "My mama told me you splattered his brains all over his trailer. Said you used a shotgun. You were just fifteen years old, so you got away with it. You claimed it was self-defense but nobody in this town believed you, and so they sent your gun-happy ass away. It took twenty years for you to work up the guts to show your face here again. You came back and waved a shit load of money around and got the best girl in town to marry you, so now everybody has to pretend to forget what you really are. I may be a thief and a piece of shit, big brother, but at least I ain't a murderer, like *you*."

Roan's hands went around Zach's throat with a speed neither I nor Zach could have predicted. Zach fell backward and Roan went with him, never letting go. They landed on the floor with Roan on top of him. Zach struggled and choked. His face began turning bright red.

"Freddie, get help!" I yelled.

"It's coming. Arnie! Arnie!"

I fell to my knees beside Roan and tried to pry his fingers off Zach's convulsing throat. "Roan, let go of him. Roan, stop."

But Roan looked down at his gasping, choking brother with sheer fury. Through gritted teeth he said, "I'd be . . . doing the world . . . a favor."

"Not this time. Stop."

Zach finally managed to latch both handcuffed hands onto Roan's left forearm, the one nearest me. Zach shoved hard at precisely the moment Roan decided to let go of him. Roan's left arm was flung backwards with the elbow bent.

That elbow hit me squarely in the face.

LOVE MEANS NEVER having to say you're sorry for accidentally giving your wife a black eye during a prison smackdown. That's what it means to me at least. Roan, however, looked miserable beside me in a darkened cubicle of Dunderry Regional's emergency room. His arm made a rigid brace around my waist. I leaned against him in an obvious show of forgiveness that didn't soften his jaw. I held an ice pack to my eye.

Standing nearby in a yellow bunny suit, cousin Violet looked from me to him worriedly, her yellow ears waggling like strange antennae. Violet was that rarest of creatures: part physical therapist, part storyteller, part bunny. She'd been up in the pediatrics ward when we came in, reading Beatrix Potter to the kids.

"Sonny's on the way down?" I asked her. "With the baby?"

She sighed and nodded.

"No fractures," the young ER doctor confirmed as she clipped my x-rays to a screen. She was also that rarest of creatures: a non-relative.

The hospital had imported her from Florida. It's always good to diversify the gene pool. "So Claire, you can go on home. Just keep some ice on the eye, take some aspirin, and enjoy the rainbow colors of the bruises you'll have for the next three or four weeks." She glanced up furtively at the blue and magenta splotches on Roan's face. "I guess y'all know what to expect."

He studied the x-rays without a hint of relief. "I wish we didn't."

"Not your fault," I said again, patting his hand on my hip.

"Not your fault, Roan," Violet added, nodding fervently. Her ears flopped in unison.

"Oh? My wife has a bruise the size of my elbow on her face." His shoulders sagged.

I tugged his hand. "Let's go see Zach." Violet waddled after us, wringing her paws, as we walked to the nurses' station. Alvin headed us off before we got to Freddie and Arnie at the cubicle across the way. Alvin's scowl was as dark as his Sunday suit. Nothing makes a Baptist deacon madder than leaving church to play referee for hopeless sinners and a physical therapist in a bunny suit.

"That boy's trouble. No more face-to-face meetings."

"I take responsibility for what happened."

"Freddie told me what he said to provoke you."

"That's no excuse."

Alvin glanced around, then stepped closer to us and spoke in a low voice. "Roan, there's the law and then there's justice. That boy doesn't want nor deserve your help. Think what could happen if you set him free in this community. Not just what you might end up doing to him, but what he might end up doing to your friends, your family, your neighbors." Alvin's voice dropped lower. "Leave him to the system. One thing can lead to another, understand? The state of Georgia can make sure he's locked up for a long, long time." Alvin looked at me. "Josh and I have talked this over."

Roan said nothing. He stared at the door to Zach's exam room, a muscle flexing in his jaw. I lowered my ice pack. Alvin winced at my eye. It was swollen shut. "Claire, I don't like the look in your good eye."

Head up, eye twitching, I stepped away from the group. "I'm going in that cubicle and speak to the human being who I call Zach Sullivan. Because he is Roan's half-brother, and therefore, my . . . half brother-in-law." I stared at Violet so hard her ears nearly drooped. "Your cousin-in-law." And then at Alvin. "And yours, too, whether you want to admit it or not."

Finally I looked up at Roan. "He's knows how to push your

buttons, but you don't have to let him do it. I don't blame you for trying to throttle him, and I certainly don't blame you for my eye, but if you need to walk in that room right now and at least *try* to talk to him."

Roan looked at me with more misery and tenderness than I can describe. Defeat cut grooves around his mouth. He nodded.

I followed him into the exam room. Freddie and Arnie gaped at us but stepped aside. What we saw on the exam table made us stop quickly. Zach didn't notice us. There he sat in his orange jumpsuit, bound in ankle chains and handcuffs, the handcuffs attached to a chain around his waist, his neck already swelling where Roan had bruised his windpipe. He bent his head over Forsythia, who he cuddled in the crook of his left arm. He managed to lift his big-knuckled right hand high enough to waggle a forefinger before her eyes. She smiled then reached up one tiny hand and grasped his finger.

Supervising from a few feet away, Sonny waved a yellow wing at us. He'd been assisting Violet in her storytelling rounds. He was dressed as a duck, or rather, as a pediatric nurse duck, since he'd covered his costume in a sterile paper gown.

Zach looked up. Before he hid behind a mask I glimpsed a sweetness no one could deny. Maybe he didn't have enough spiritual sugar to survive, but the potential was there. We watched a dozen emotions cross his face before grim determination won out. "You take her," he said to Roan, his voice a rasp. His throat was raw from the inside out. "That's all I care about. Be good to her. Give her a good home. You and me ain't cut out to be brothers, not real ones, but that ain't her fault."

Roan crossed his arms and bowed his head in contemplation. His eyes were half-shut. He'd taught me that armored squint; it pared down the surroundings to one narrow laser beam of truth at a time. He spoke slowly, as if every word might end the world. "*What do you want to do with your life*?"

Zach blinked in surprise then scowled. "Is that a trick question?"

"Answer me."

He swallowed hard. "Stay out of prison." He paused, thinking hard. "Get rich." Another pause. His sarcastic smile returned. "Like my big brother."

"What kind of work can you do?"

"Anything that takes two hands and a strong back."

"Then why haven't you done it already?"

"Because I was stupid and looked for easy pickings instead."

"What happens the next time you get a choice between easy and hard?"

"I hope I pick the pickings that don't put me back in prison."

At least he admitted that much. I realized the rest might be sweet talk, and so did Roan. I watched my husband agonize in silence. A part of me wished he'd put his foot down—act like a domineering prick, tell me I was naïve and this stranger would only break our hearts.

No, we are not taking responsibility for this criminal. I'm the man of this family, and that's my final word on the subject.

Roan would thus absolve me of responsibility for abandoning Zach, and yet I'd still have a shot at snatching custody of Forsythia. Most women don't want a return of the old fashioned male-female power system, but *I can't do it because my husband won't let me* still comes in handy as an excuse.

At least I admitted that much.

Roan exhaled. He lifted one hand. He counted on his fingers. "One. You sign over custody of the baby to me and my wife. Two. I drop the assault charges and pay off your debts and fines, which probably means you can qualify for parole sometime this spring. Three. You play by my rules. You live where I tell you to live, you work for me, you stay out of trouble. Four. If you don't do all of the above, I'll make sure you're back in jail before you can spit. And I'll walk away without looking back."

Silence. A staring match. Zach laughed, a grotesque sound. His throat was covered in welts from Roan's fingers. "Man, you'll be on the look-out for any excuse to put me away for good. I won't stand a chance."

"Take it or leave it."

Long pause. I held my breath. Zach looked down at the baby. Forsythia smiled up at him. "As part of this deal, will I get to see her a lot?"

"As long as you hold up your part of that deal. Like I said, take it or leave it."

He hooked his finger gently, jiggling the small hand that refused to let go. A passion for fatherhood often comes on quickly and unexpectedly, like miracles and religious conversions and UFO abductions. Zach looked at the small, brown hand that clutched his with such determination.

"I'll take it," he said.

If only it had turned out to be that simple.

6

AND SO OUR fates were cast. The consequences immediately crept out of their burrows and bared their teeth at us like an Easter bunny with a hangover. During the two weeks leading up to the spring's biggest religious and decorative-egg-hunting event Roan and I went about the business of settling Zach Donovan's criminal business and securing custody of Forsythia. The consensus of friends and family was clear.

We had lost our minds.

Plain crazy, the Methodists said when Roan reimbursed them for all their festival losses.

Gone nuts, the Kehoes said when he talked them into dropping their charges against Zach in return for a generous donation to their favorite charities.

Well-intentioned fools, suckers, and bleeding hearts, said various members of the community as Roan paid the bills for their new catalytic converters.

Asking for trouble, Alvin muttered when Roan dropped the assault charges. Zach couldn't escape jail time on general counts including disturbing the peace, but with everything else wiped off his slate he'd be out on parole by the first of May.

We had to have a plan for his rehabilitation by then.

My family's reaction went far beyond ordinary handwringing and tsk tsking. Mama and Daddy said they supported our decision but they were very worried. Hop and Evan, my preciously pragmatic brothers, wondered if Zach could be tamed with NASCAR and UGA Bulldogs football, two passions they viewed as balm for any miscreant soul. Brady was too busy to notice the family chaos, since he was commandeering plans for a strip mall down in Forsyth County, where nearly all the old farmsteads bore large signs promising FOR SALE. ZONED COMMERCIAL, as if that was something to brag about.

But Josh kept deathly quiet until Passover Sunday, while Mama, Daddy, Grandma Dottie and Amanda were down in Atlanta attending church with Brady and his family at their suburban mega-church (it had a coffee café and a Holy Tours travel club.) Josh flew back early from a legislators' golf tournament at Sea Island. Since Karen rarely came home early from a visit to her elegant coastal spawning grounds, I sensed trouble instantly.

They ambushed us at Evan's house. Hop and Evan lived within hollering distance of each other on a hundred acres of old dairy farm Great-Grandma Alice had willed to them. Their jolly, good old girl wives and robust kids roamed freely between two kitschy brick mini-mansions as if sharing chores in a small commune. Thus, the ensuing family meltdown had a sizable audience.

Josh's ruddy face turned bright red when he saw the current state of my eye, which had evolved into a bulbous shiner the exact color of a polished eggplant. He blamed Roan. "Have you lost your mind? Taking her to that damned jail to visit your damned *violent* half-brother! Allowing yourself to be provoked into a junkyard-dog brawl with Claire standing there. *Look at my sister's battered face*."

I grabbed Roan's arm. Roan said softly, "You're absolutely right. There's nothing you can say to me that's worse than what I've said to myself in the past week."

"That doesn't change the fact that it happened!"

"Josh," I began through gritted teeth. "This is none of your business."

"Baby sister, everything that happens in this family is my business."

"No, you only *think* it's your business."

"Hold on, y'all, calm yourselves down," Hop protested. "There's no need to get all riled."

"That's right," Evan said. "Claire's a big girl. She's been smacked in the snout before."

Such a way with words. My sweet middle brothers, paunchy and placid and nearing forty, got between us and formed a beefy firewall, holding out their arms like fence rails to keep Josh and Roan apart. "Joshua," Evan growled, "Now just cool off, I said. Roan, stay back."

Karen glared around Josh's tailored shoulder like an irate blonde poodle. "We came here to talk some sense into you-all. Think about what's best for the family's future, Claire."

"You mean Josh's political future."

"Baby sis, now, now," Evan begged.

Josh thrust a thick finger between Hop and Evan, jabbing it at us. "Mama and Daddy are against this crazy plan of yours but they don't want to risk alienating you and Roan, so they're agonizing over it in silence. But I'm not. I've kept quiet long enough. *This is insane*. Roan, I don't care if that criminal *is* your half-brother. He doesn't belong here and you know it. Look what's happened already, and the bastard's not even out of jail yet. If you encourage him to stay in this community you'll lose every bit of goodwill you've built up here."

Roan went absolutely still except for the sinister little smile growing on his mouth. He bound one arm around me, keeping me clenched tight to his side. Here came the revelations, the ugly admissions and whispered gossip he'd always suspected beneath the welcoming surface of my family. He smiled at Josh to provoke Josh to keep talking, and it worked.

". . . it's time to decide whether to fish or cut bait," Josh went on, now in full oratory command. "If you really want to be part of this family you'll consider this problem a *family* problem. I know Claire talks you into things; when she's on her high horse she's always trying to save the world one troubled loser at a time—"

Oh, my God. He inferred that I'd already saved one *troubled loser*—Roan—and should stop while I was ahead. Hop and Evan nearly danced with alarm. "Josh, shut the hell up and think about what you're saying," Hop yelled.

". . . and that *baby*, that mixed-race mystery baby—dear God, for all we know, her mother was some ghetto hooker up in Chattanooga. That baby probably has a whole family tree full of crack dealers and welfare queens and foul-mouthed gangbangers. She doesn't need to be left anywhere *near* her tattooed thug of a white daddy. For godssake, Roan, have more sense than Claire. Don't think of this Donovan and his rug rat as blood kin of yours. Do you really want to fight a *new* battle over the reputation of the Sullivan name? It took you long enough to salvage it last time."

Hop and Evan dropped their arms and simply gaped at our older brother in distress. They couldn't save him, us, or the family from the bitter hole he kept digging. I felt sick at my stomach. When I looked up at Roan, he had tilted his head to one side and regarded Josh with a kind of harsh wonder, his eyes predatory and steel gray.

Karen, the idiot, popped from behind Josh in a flurry of blue cashmere and seed pearls. "Now look, Claire, have some sympathy. Your brother's campaign advisors are already worried about his family image. We're going to have do some fancy tap dancing around the unfortunate issue of Matthew's beginnings as a . . . a *love child* with one of the local whores."

She gave Josh a quick hug. "I'm sorry, sweetie, but we have to talk turkey about your political liabilities. You've got one illegitimate son and as for your daughter, well, Amanda is just an unpredictable little social *retard*, bless her heart."

She glared at Roan and me. "You see? We're working with a lot of negatives for Josh's family image. The whole law-and-order thing is a key platform issue for him, and how it going to look when he says we have to get tough on low-lifes like Donovan and then it turns out Donovan's part of the family!" She wagged a finger. "You all do realize that Zach Donovan's mother and Matthew's mother were sisters, and that means Matthew and Zach are first cousins, and that means Josh is that white trash criminal's *uncle*, his uncle! My lord! But you two are just so selfish you don't even think about how that looks! You are intent on making a public spectacle of us all!"

Even Josh looked a little deflated and regretful now. He'd stood there and let his trophy wife hold up an ugly mirror that reflected more than she suspected about his mistakes and foibles.

But he'd dug this pit, so now I let him wallow in it.

Roan looked down at me. "You say whatever you need to say. I'll be outside."

He walked out.

I looked at Josh. He held out a hand. "Baby Sis, none of that came out quite the way I intended—"

"It's exactly what you intended," I said quietly. "Stay away from me. Stay away from Roan. Stay away from Zach Donovan, and you better damn sure stay away from the baby. We don't need your approval, and we don't want your approval, and I'm ashamed to be your sister."

I joined Roan in the yard. It was strewn with toys, go-carts, swing sets, lost video game controls, and lifelike plastic deer the Hop/Evan children practiced shooting with BB guns. I'll take an honest appetite for carnage over a fake claim of piety, any day. Roan leaned against his Jeep, watching me intently.

I was nearly crying, and it takes a lot to make me bawl. I wound a hand through his. "You only agreed to live in Dunderry for my sake. If you want to move back to Oregon, where you were happy for twenty years, I'm ready to go."

His face compressed in sad appreciation of my heartfelt lie. "We'll see this through right here, where it started," he said. "And decide what to do after that."

So the door was open to leave my family and our hometown behind.

(Please continue reading for more information)

Coming in Summer 2014:

Part Two of *Where the Foxgloves Bloom*

To subscribe to Deb's blog for updates, drop her a note at
deborahsmithauthor@gmail.com

Thank you so much for asking about this sequel and waiting patiently. I'm trying my best to get back to what I do best—writing the books I love.

Your interest in those books means the world to me.

Fondly,
—*Deb*

About the Author:
Deborah Smith

Deborah Smith is the author of 35 novels in romance and women's fiction, including the *New York Times* bestseller, *A Place To Call Home*, and the Number 1 Kindle bestseller, *The Crossroads Café*. RT Magazine named *A Place To Call Home* one of the Top 200 Romances of the 20th Century. In 2006, *Library Journal* named *The Crossroads Café* one of the top romances of the year. Since 2000, Deborah has is co-founder, partner, vice president and editor in chief at BelleBooks, a small publishing house that now includes the imprints Bell Bridge Books and ImaJinn Books. As a writer, Deborah is currently working on novellas and short stories spun off from *The Crossroads Café*. The newest story is *The Yarn Spinner*, January 2014. She lives in the mountains of north Georgia with her husband, six cats and two dogs; all rescues. (Not her husband.)

Made in the USA
Middletown, DE
10 April 2016